THE HEAD AND THE HEART

FATED:
EROS AND PSYCHE

DRAGONFIRE PRESS

OTHER BOOKS

Fated

The Head and the Heart

The Flower and the Flame

The Sorrow and the Sea

Cursed

The Princess and the Prophecy

The Fallow and the Faint

The Weaver and the Web

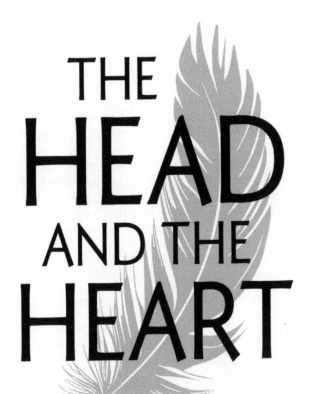

THE
HEAD
AND THE
HEART

FATED:
EROS AND PSYCHE

KERRI KEBERLY

The Head and the Heart
Copyright © 2021 by Kerri Keberly

This is a work of fiction. All events portrayed in this
book are fictitious, and any resemblance to real people
or events is purely coincidental.

Cover design by Keith Robinson

Dragonfire Press

Print ISBN: 978-1-958354-66-7

Originally published in March 2021

Second Edition: 2024

CHAPTER 1

PSYCHE WAS CURSED, so it was only fitting the veil of her headdress be as black as the River Styx on her wedding day. Her husband was to be a winged beast. The Oracle of Delphi had foretold it. Most convenient, then, she was appropriately dressed for what would surely also be her funeral.

The wind moaned low and mournful, and she clutched the edges of her cloak, wrapping herself tighter within its folds. Her mother had dyed it to match her veil, and the wedding dress she wore, pinned with onyx set in gold, was the same shade of despair.

She wondered how much longer she would have to wait for her groom to arrive. Exactly how many hours she had been shivering on the mountaintop she didn't know. Long enough for the Earth to swallow down the sun and cast up the moon in its place.

Would the beast's wings be immense and leathery or small and scaly? The prophecy hadn't revealed what they would look like, only that it would have them. Truth be told she no longer cared. As long as her family remained safe, she would make the sacrifice—*be* the sacrifice. That it had come to this was her fault, after all.

1

"Gods above, please let death take me quickly," she murmured yet another prayer aloud. "Grant me that much at least."

Cold from the large stone beneath her seeped through cloak and skin, then finally, into her bones. Another round of shivering pitched her forward, her back aching in protest. The weight of her headdress made her head throb. She longed to take it off, but if there was one thing she'd learned from her twenty summers on Earth, it was that her parents would march back up the mountain to choke the life out of her themselves if she didn't make a good impression. Being handed over to a beast or not, she was a princess. Therefore, the headdress would stay on, at least until after the ceremony... If there even was a ceremony.

She adjusted into a more comfortable position and continued to wait. Not how she imagined her wedding night—sore and trembling in the arms of a cold and indifferent night—but she had been given no other choice.

An owl questioned soft and low from within the spiky shadows of a pine tree: Who? Who? Who?

She pulled in a breath, and when her eyes began to sting along with the burning in her lungs, she realized air wasn't the only thing she was refusing to let go. Her throat ached from the fight to keep the tears lurking behind her eyes at bay.

Me, me, me. I'm the one betrothed to a monster.

The moonlight illuminated the ground until it fell away to nothing, and her watery eyes followed the length of the rocky ledge just a few feet away. How fitting she sat so close to the edge of a dark and terrifying abyss. Metaphorical, even. Perhaps she should give herself over to the jagged rocks below and be done with it.

No. The prophecy must come to pass.

How had it come to this? Waiting on the summit of a mountain in the dead of night for a beast to claim her as its wife. She'd had plenty of suitors, and only months ago. They'd come to her father's kingdom in droves, bringing gifts of gold and silver, sparkling jewels to detract from their ogling eyes, lolling tongues, and lustful intentions. Her renowned beauty had drawn them from far and wide to worship at her feet. Until eight full moons ago, when they had suddenly stopped coming.

They gave up because you were too irreverent, her sisters had said. *But none of their hearts felt true*, she'd replied. If only she knew then what she knew now. She would have accepted an offer while she'd had the chance.

Both her parents had been determined to arrange a marriage, even if it would have been a loveless one, into a family as wealthy and high in status, as royalty is wont to do. In the early days, her prospects had seemed endless. But she hadn't cared for the attention and refused them all. Now she wished her father had forced her to choose. He'd been biding his

3

time for different reasons, counting on the beauty and grace that preceded her to attract a more extravagant suitor than the next.

Her father was a clever man; waiting for the right opportunity to present itself had always done him well when it came to both his riches and his rise to power. When it had come to the marriage of his youngest, most beautiful daughter, however, he had played a fool's hand.

No one, not even a king, could have known how much the unadulterated worship and adoration would upset Aphrodite, goddess of love and beauty. Not until it was too late.

Your beauty has angered the gods, daughter, her father had proclaimed. *We've been cursed! Who will marry you now?*

Not long after, he'd dragged her to see the Pythia, the high priestess of the Temple of Apollo, to confirm his suspicions. He had been right. She had been born too fair of skin and pure of heart for her own good—he too concerned with an advantageous alliance for his—and it would cost them all.

Let Psyche's body be clad in mourning wed, the blind old seer had spat out over her divining stones, the flames from the brazier reflecting in her milky eyes as her trance rocked her back and forth. *Her husband is no being of human seed, but serpent dire and fierce as might be thought. Who flies with wings above in starry skies, and doth subdue each thing with fiery flight...*

Serpent. Wings. Fire. The words echoed in Psyche's head as she pulled her knees to her chest and rested her sandaled heels on the edge of the stone. Improper for a king's daughter, but there was no one there to stop her. How ironic she should gain the freedom to break the rules of propriety by having her hands so cruelly tied.

Her parents had brought her up here, wailing and sobbing, knowing they would never see her again. The procession had been long and included some of the city's most prominent members. They had dressed her in black as instructed by the oracle, and then escorted her to the top of the mountain only to abandon her.

She knew they hadn't had a choice, but resentment still set her jaw and ground her teeth. She hadn't asked for alluring eyes, silken hair, or such a pleasing form. It could be helped no more than a songbird could help singing. Yet, as unfair as it was, there was nothing they could do but see the goddess whom Psyche had angered appeased. To knowingly and willingly change the course of foreseen events was utter lunacy. Meddling with prophecy meant certain doom. The gods would seek revenge, seeing to it that ruin befell the entire family.

So, she sat, hunched on a rock freezing under the silvery moon and passing the time pondering the beast's wings and her fate while counting stars. What did it matter how her life ended now anyway, on the rocks below or in the razor-sharp talons of a ferocious winged serpent? It would be over soon enough, and she'd be glad for it.

A breeze lifted the wisps that had escaped the confines of her elaborately plaited hair. It washed over her, carrying with it the faint scent of wild roses. The hem of her cloak flapped as the wind gathered strength. Sand hissed around her jeweled feet, now firmly planted on the ground where she stood with her fists clenched tight, ready to face the beast head on.

"Psyche."

The voice drew a startle out of her. It sounded like a gentle-natured man, soothing, not snarling as one might expect. Most curiously, it hadn't come from in front of her or behind, but all around.

She peered into the darkness surrounding her. Surely it was some kind of sorcery performed by her beastly husband-to-be to trick her into a false sense of calm. To lure her to it, where it waited deep within the jutting layers of rock.

"I am here." Her own voice wavered, its pitch pulled high and tight as she forced herself to answer.

"Do not be afraid."

She swayed on her feet, both fear and annoyance making her heart pound and her palms sweat. Was this command supposed to put her mind at ease? Such things were not so simple.

"Easier said than done. It is not you alone on a mountaintop in the middle of the night waiting to be dragged away by a monster!"

A whistling gust of laughter ruffled the surrounding mountain brush's papery leaves. "I am not a beast, dear girl, I am Zephyrus, called upon to carry you to your betrothed."

Zephyrus was the god of the west wind, the warm and gentle breeze that ushered in spring. Her insolence fell away, replaced by awe as she dropped to her knees and bowed her head.

"Forgive me."

Hope filled her. If the beast was favored enough by Zephyrus that the god would agree to do its bidding, how terrible could it be? Did this mean it was capable of mercy? Could she convince it to let her return to her family?

Perhaps... if only it doesn't devour me first.

The wind god's warmth settled around her like reassuring arms upon her shoulders, giving her just enough courage to lift her head. "Whatever has called upon you, benevolent Zephyrus, would it treat me as kindly as you?"

The breeze picked up, quickly spiraling into a whirlwind that billowed the fabric of her cloak and dress, her question forgotten when a powerful rush of air lifted her off her feet.

The wind grew in strength until her arms flailed and her hands grasped for purchase, groping desperately though there was none to be had. As if pulled by invisible strings, her chest raised first, then her legs, until she was lying on her back, floating on air. A small gasp escaped as she marveled at her wingless flight, her cloak and hair rippling lazily around her as if submerged in a pool of dark water. Cradled in weightless warmth, her eyelids began to close, the heaviness of her tears unbearable as she finally let them fall.

"Shhh." The west wind blew, lulling her into a deep and dreamless sleep.

CHAPTER 2

THIN BLADES OF grass caressed Psyche's cheek, rousing her from slumber. She blinked the sky into view; it was a breathtaking blue, cloudless and painted in a shade she could not find the words to describe.

After propping herself up on her elbows, she surveyed her surroundings—a small meadow, dotted with wildflowers and enclosed on three sides with trees. The babbling from a nearby brook conversed with a neighboring songbird, both informing her it was a good morning.

Psyche rolled onto all fours before sitting on her heels. The black fabric of her wedding dress looked a dull and dirty brown in the dazzling light, but a warm breeze made up for the sad sight by rippling the tall grass like waves on the sea.

She clasped her hands together. "Oh, mighty Zephyrus... Take me home, I beg of you!" She closed her eyes and lifted her chin, waiting to be carried back to the mountaintop.

When the wind god did not answer her prayer, she opened her eyes and watched the grass sway in silence. Moments later, when the breeze faded and the grass stilled, there came a whisper, "I cannot. This is your fate, dear girl. Go to him. He will not deny you... but dare not break his trust, for it will cost you much."

Psyche's throat swelled, the confirmation she had not yet fulfilled the prophecy bearing down on her already heavy heart. She removed the pins of her headdress and threw them to the ground, her brow grooving deeply as she did so. She was to go to the beast, that much was clear, but had Zephyrus revealed there might be a chance she could persuade the beast to let her live, or perhaps even let her go? She sighed, suddenly exhausted. Why did the gods speak in such riddles and rhymes?

A rustling from the edge of the trees startled her, and she tossed her headdress aside to crouch low in the grass. She tried to keep her breath steady, but the heart racing in her chest had other ideas. Something moved from within the shadows and, barely breathing, she clamped her teeth down on the inside of her bottom lip to keep from bleating out in fear.

A snow-white doe emerged from the forest and stepped into the clearing. She trained her red eyes in Psyche's direction and sniffed the air, stretching her neck up and outward. Relieved it wasn't the beast, impatient and come to claim his due in a fury of fangs and claws, Psyche eased the air out of her lungs, managing not to move a muscle though her limbs quaked uncontrollably.

The doe swiveled her head toward the end of the meadow that wasn't lined with trees. Ears pricked forward, she stared off into the distance. Turning her head toward Psyche again, their eyes met. The doe's unsettling from the absence of color, yet hauntingly beautiful. Psyche inhaled a deep, stuttering breath, her own eyes filling with tears.

She'd kept her end of the bargain. She'd sat and waited, resisting the urge to jump off the mountain, and the gods had decided to repay her sacrifice by delaying her agony. Adding insult to injury, she must go to *it*, the beast, to end this misery. The least the gods could have done was get it over with, not show her one last bit of beauty in the world before taking it all away.

The doe stamped her foot, scattering Psyche's thoughts. The ethereal animal turned her head toward the open end of the meadow again, and this time, Psyche followed her gaze. In the distance was the very tip of an immense cornice and pediment. The doe began to move with deliberate steps, one after another, delicately picking her way through small blue flowers.

Follow her.

The voice inside her head sent Psyche clambering to her feet. She rose to her full height, which was a palm higher than both of her sisters, who were taller than most. When she spied a magnificent palace, even grander than her father's, towering in the distance, she gulped down the sick feeling rising from her belly. Unless the goddess whom she'd offended took pity on her, she would die at the hands of a winged serpent before nightfall.

Psyche lifted her tattered and somber skirts above her ankles and followed after the doe. A butterfly bounced alongside her, and with each step she took, more of them gathered; a cloud of fluttering wings following her every move. She lifted her arm and dozens settled on her wrist, in the crook of her bare arm, and in her hair. Their soft wings tickled her skin, and she silently thanked the tiny souls for the comfort they offered.

When she finally reached the palace, an expansive courtyard of white granite, glittering like diamonds in the sunlight, stretched out before her. She made her way up a set of wide stairs, passing between two of the many columns that surrounded the palace and proceeding under the porch that covered the entrance. The massive and intricately carved arched doors swung open before she could raise a fist to knock.

Terror lashed through her, knocking her knees. No matter how grand this palace was, or how peaceful the meadow seemed, she knew she was about to come face-to-face with a nightmare.

She felt herself fading, on the verge of falling, when a voice pulled her up from the dark.

"I've been waiting for you." It was the same voice that had spoken earlier, urging her to follow the doe. It was warm and honeyed like the west wind, but deeper. Smooth and calming, not treacherous. "Come in."

But sounds could be deceiving, and she reminded herself the voice belonged to a monster. A winged beast hidden somewhere within the shadowy recesses of this beautiful palace—and the only chance she had at ever seeing her family again.

She closed her eyes and stepped over the threshold.

The seconds ticked by like endless days. When she heard no snapping teeth or raking claws, only the sound of her own ragged breathing, she opened one lid. No beast. She opened the other and discovered a wonder of luxury and riches unimaginable.

More columns held up carved arches, and in the center of the enormous entryway, a fountain, featuring crystal clear water dribbling from a small urn held by a winged cherub. Between some of the columns, marble statues looked on from atop stone pedestals. She gasped in wonder at the enormous golden chandeliers hanging from the coffered ceiling and the tiled floor inlaid with precious gems that lay beneath her feet.

"You approve."

Panic clawed its way up her spine, and the hair on the nape of her neck stood on end. She had surveyed her surroundings thoroughly and was quite sure she had seen no one else in the room.

"Don't be frightened."

Despite the request, her legs began to buckle, and her throat tightened as she fought against the blackness once again closing in on all sides.

He must desire slashing through a beating heart. This was the only reason she could think of as to why he'd made himself invisible. If her heart stopped from laying eyes upon his terrifying nature, he would not enjoy the thrill of killing her as much. At least she wouldn't have to endure the sight of his hideous face, only the pain of his sharp claws as he tore her apart.

She swayed as she spoke the only words that mattered to her now, quickly before it was too late. "I have kept my end of the..." Her hands groped for something—anything—to keep her from falling.

"You have. Your family is safe."

She dropped to her knees, fingers splayed outward to keep the little balance she had left, before crumpling into a heap. The beast had decided to accept his offering after all. Her family would live, and she could die with that peace of mind.

The cool tiles felt heavenly against her flaming cheek. When she finally opened her eyes, she focused her gaze on the base of the fountain, so that she wouldn't faint again. Her mouth went slack with disbelief when she heard the voice say, "There is a bath near your rooms. Why don't you relax? Perhaps rest for a while? When you're feeling up to it, we'll feast in honor of your arrival."

The thoughtful words floated down around her soft as rose petals, and her head spun with the madness of it all. How could she possibly reconcile the image of the ferocious face in her mind with the sweet voice in her ears?

After a few moments of silence, she felt fingers brush away the hair that had fallen across her face. She stiffened when sturdy hands wrapped around her shoulders, gently urging her to rise. She saw nothing, but the warmth of flesh and the solidness of bone upon her own skin were unmistakable. It made her shiver, and when her hands groped for balance, they found it on a pair of lean and muscled forearms.

Not fur. Not cold, hard scales. Warm, smooth skin. It must be a trick, a ruse to calm her. Perhaps *she* was the feast and fear toughened the flesh.

An invisible hand enveloped hers, waiting until she caught her breath before pulling her toward the arched stone entrance into the east wing. Psyche let herself be led, not daring to resist.

"Straight ahead is the dining room, which leads to the gardens," said the voice, without any hint of malice. "The library and kitchen are on either side, and the rooms in the east wing are for you. Feel free to roam anywhere on the grounds you wish... all except for the west wing. The west wing is forbidden."

Psyche nodded, calmer in knowing the beast planned to keep her around long enough to give her boundaries. Although she didn't see herself venturing too far from her rooms, she thought it a good sign.

Still, she couldn't help but ask, "How long do I have?"

The hand released her, dragging clawless fingertips along her palm. "Take all the time you need. We'll celebrate your arrival whenever you are ready."

Celebrate? She'd been asking how long she had left to live.

"Thank you." She bowed her head, silently blowing a sigh from between parted lips.

She walked on shaky legs down the hall, contemplating her next move. It seemed as though he was not intent on devouring her body and soul, at least not until after she was properly rested. Now was the time to use the wits the gods had given her. If what the seer said was true, if he truly was as powerful as the gods, and if he had a penchant for fiery flight as predicted, she must appear honored to be his guest or it would only be a matter of time before she wore out her welcome. She would dine with the beast tonight, and every night until she figured out how to escape his clutches unscathed.

"Psyche," said the voice, making her stop in her tracks. "I look forward to your company. Please be sure to bring your friends."

Her eyebrows pulled together as she craned her neck to look behind first one shoulder and then the other. She was still alone as far as she could tell.

Psyche's gaze darted about, desperate to connect the voice to a shape. She waited expectantly for an explanation but received none.

When she saw the butterflies flitting around her head, she couldn't help but smile.

CHAPTER 3

THE WEDDING DRESS dropped onto the stone tiles, and Psyche was glad to be rid of it. Sinking into the hot bath, she sighed. Whatever fight lie ahead, as cunning and ruthless as the beast would turn out to be, there was no turning back.

The deal had been struck between the beast and the gods. She was his now and must keep her head if she was ever to see home again. At least for the time being, it seemed as though the beast thought more of her comfort than the taste of her blood.

Though tempted, she found the churning in her belly would not allow her to languish in the steaming water, so she bathed quickly and dried with a length of linen before a fire burning in a stone hearth.

Her eyes glanced over an expanse of fine russet-colored silk draped across the sleeping sofa. The edges of the beautiful garment were embroidered in black and gold thread, resembling the pattern on the wings of a butterfly.

She marveled at the perfection of the needlework. After folding and pinning the *peplos* into place, she attempted to re-plait her hair but stopped halfway through the ordeal. Why bother? She never liked sitting through the countless hours it took for her sisters to complete those elaborate hairstyles anyway. Her heart wrenched at the thought. She'd always hated their constant lecturing, but now she missed it.

Hair tousled free, she picked up an ivory comb from a small dressing table nearby and ran it through the long strands. The least she could do, she supposed, was make them proud by smoothing the waves until they shined.

Once ready, she left her chamber and made her way back toward the center of the palace to find the dining room. She let her nose lead the way, and the closer she got, the stronger the scent of spices, roasted vegetables, basted meats and freshly baked bread. The delicious aromas made her stomach rumble in anticipation, and when she found the source, she entered the room to find a great feast laid out before her.

The voice greeted her. "You must be famished. Please, sit."

A chair slid out from the table, as if by an invisible attendant. Psyche's eyes widened, but she quickly regained her composure and settled herself onto its cushioned seat. She couldn't very well bargain for her freedom while visibly shaking.

"That color suits you," said the voice. "Much better than black, wouldn't you agree? Why your parents dressed you as if you were going to a funeral, I can't quite figure out."

She looked in the direction from which the voice came, swallowing hard when her eyes connected with a great glowing mass. It held the faintest outline of a man sitting in a gilded chair at the head of the table. Yet, she could make out no discernable features, save for two arches curving and pointing high above where she knew a head should be.

Were they horns or wings? Both perhaps.

"It was part of the prophecy." She dropped her gaze to a polished silver plate sitting on the table. "That I be dressed in black. I was to have a wedding and a funeral on the same day, was I not?"

The beast did not respond. Thankfully, his presence did not turn menacing, nor did she feel threatened when he rose from the chair. Despite this, the breath in her lungs became

20

scarce when he began to move closer. She kept her gaze fixed on the plate in front of her as he glided past the back of her chair, heat sliding across her skin as he passed. When the radiant light stopped at her side and lifted the plate, making it appear as though it was floating in mid-air, she bit back a scream.

"Mm, yes, the prophecy."

Psyche watched fruit, meat and bread heap itself onto the plate. "They were concerned because..." Her voice sounded thin and desperate to her ears. "Because..."

"The proposals of marriage stopped."

She clenched her fingers tighter in her lap. "Yes."

The beast set the food before her like an offering. "You think you are at fault for the actions of others?"

"Who else is to blame? They worshiped me, turning away from the goddess of beauty and letting the flames in her temples cool to ashes, leaving the offerings of apples and roses to wither and rot. Don't you see? It *is* my fault. I did not choose."

The beast moved around the table soundlessly, and she waited to continue until he lowered himself into a chair across from her.

21

"I let them come, foolishly wanting—*waiting*—to marry for love, and Aphrodite saw to it that I pay the price for my selfishness, willing it so that no man should desire me." She explained in earnest until, forgetting herself, indignation sharpened her tongue. "Cursing me so only the foulest, most treacherous beast would take me as a bride."

Again, the beast remained silent. No pounding fists or ferocious growl at the slight, only silence, heavy and aching with something that felt like sorrow.

She bowed her head, squirming in the absence of his response and regretting her harsh choice of words. He hadn't been foul or treacherous or anything of the sort since she'd arrived. In fact, he had been nothing but gracious and hospitable and kind.

"It was not your fault," said the beast when he finally spoke. "Vanity is a weakness, even for the goddess of love and beauty. And the Pythia sees only what Apollo allows. He is proud and petulant, one who does not take defeat lightly. When gods conspire, mortals suffer. You were not supposed to be dressed for a funeral, Psyche, only a wedding."

Her breath hitched. Thoroughly caught between terror at what destruction a creature

22

like the beast was capable of and disarmed by the wisdom and sweet temperament of his voice, she suddenly wished to see the lips that uttered her name so softly. She wanted to see him in his own flesh, no matter how terrible, not blurred behind a veil of light meant to keep her blind to his likeness.

She had wanted to scream earlier, but now she wanted to wail. How was she supposed to reconcile these vast differences? The task was too difficult, at least for now, and so she chose to form her own image of him in her mind, picturing a young man, with curling hair and expressive eyes.

"The oracle said you were a beast." She held on to the image that gave her the courage to ask her questions. "Yet you speak kindly, as though you are a wise father or a smitten lover, but certainly not a beast. You also speak as if you are privy to the thoughts and wills of the gods. Tell me..." She faltered, searching for something to call him other than a beast. It didn't seem right now that she sat as an honored guest at his table. "What shall I call you?"

"Syzygos?" *Husband?*

"Tell me, syzygos," she continued, smiling politely. There was no reason to disagree, after all. "Were you once a mortal man or were you born a winged beast, fashioned of fire and iron by the gods to wreak havoc upon the Earth?"

"I supposed that is one way to think of it. Although, I prefer to say I was fashioned of love and hate. I am no man, Psyche, but let us not speak of that. Such things do not matter. Fate has seen to it that you still live and breathe by my hand, against great odds. I know you wish it so, but you can never gaze upon my face, or know the truth of my being. Take comfort in knowing that you shall have all you need here, and more. I will give it freely. As terrible of a beast as I may seem, I do possess a heart, and it longs to take care of you. Let that be enough."

Psyche's shoulders sank, with despair or relief she did not know, perhaps a little of both. The last of the hope she could talk the beast into releasing her drained away, and, most strangely, in its place arose a longing to match his.

"Please, enjoy the food," he said, gently steering the conversation in a different direction. "How about some wine?"

A golden ruby-encrusted goblet appeared on the table before her, and she reached for it with tears in her eyes. How strange he always seemed to know the right words to say.

The wine tasted sweet, like nectar fit for the gods, and she found she could not stop drinking. After she had consumed a considerable amount, and the moments of silence it bought her were spent, she spoke.

"I hope I've not offended you by calling you hideous. If it would be known, you seem quite companionable, and I am most grateful that you have spared my life. I don't know that I will ever stop missing my family, but I will try... to be happy here."

He released a puff of air, in which she heard both relief and elation, and it pleased her. She was heartened by him; by his tenderness, and she thought perhaps they could find solace in each other's company, tending their wounds of loneliness and loss together.

"I'm happy to hear you say so," he said, the halo surrounding him flaring the slightest bit. "Now, tell me the things that please you most, Psyche. I want to hear all there is to know."

CHAPTER 4

As HAD BECOME their routine, Psyche and her *syzygos* had conversed well into the morning the night before. He had made good on his word, learning everything there was to know about her, from how she acquired the jagged scar on her knee to her penchant for overthinking almost everything. Only when the candles were little more than twisted ropes of melted wax dripping down the candelabra, and several yawns had managed to break free, did he bid her good night.

Once satisfied she wouldn't end up a midnight meal, it hadn't taken long to grow comfortable enough to explore. In the mornings, the gardens or the forest, and in the afternoons, she nibbled on the ripest, tastiest fruit while reading scrolls filled with lessons usually reserved for men.

It was fascinating how they thought, men. More curious than fascinating, she decided, that they kept their philosophies and calculations hidden away from the eyes of women, who, sadly, were more than happy to work their hands to the bone with household duty in exchange. Speaking of household duties, she even enjoyed the loom now that she wasn't forced to sit and learn to work it.

Despite keeping herself busy, she found that she looked forward to each evening, when her *syzygos* came back. Where he went during the day, she did not know, and she did not inquire. They hadn't been formally married, with the required ceremony and vows, and so she did not think it her place to ask. Time would tell if his favor would wane, but for now he was proving there was no one above her, and she would not speed the arrival of its end by demanding every moment of his time.

She would simply be glad for the evenings, when she could hear his voice after the silence of the day. Birds and wind and waves were not unpleasant sounds, very lovely companions indeed, but she craved breath and words and laughter.

She caught herself many times each day thinking about the moments after he would say it was time to retire. How she waited nervously—or was it breathlessly?—as he walked her to the entrance of the east wing, wondering if he would ask to follow her to her chambers, or retreat in a shimmering mist of light down the corridor of the west wing to his own rooms yet again.

On this morning, the sun shined brightly, and the clouds rolled by lazily, pure white against cerulean skies. Psyche sat up to stretch off the remnants of sleep but instead froze at the sound of giggling.

Her *syzyzgos* laughed, and he occasionally chuckled, but he did not giggle.

"Finally! She's awake!" exclaimed a voice. It was female, young and spritely.

Psyche pulled the covers to her chin protectively, her gaze darting around the room to find the culprit. She saw nothing but a trio of butterflies flitting about, which wasn't all that unusual since she seemed to attract them wherever she went.

"Heavens, you've gone and startled her." Another female voice, stern sounding and middling in age, reprimanded the first.

"Who are you? *Where* are you?" Psyche demanded answers, even though she knew not seeing wasn't necessarily grounds for not believing. Not here, in the place where voices did not belong to bodies.

The stern voice spoke once more. "You can see us..."

Psyche scanned the room again for additional occupants. Her confused glare prompted the stern voice to sputter, "Oh for the—For the love of the gods! We're right in front of you!"

"All I see are three butterflies," said Psyche. "Beautiful, surely, but certainly not possessing a mouth for speaking."

One of the butterflies, a large blue one, tumbled wildly upwards. "Oh, thank you, fair mistress, for saying we are beautiful."

A third voice, that of an old woman, said, "Yes, yes, good morning, mistress. It's the master's will for us to serve you, so we've all three been given conscious thought. It is because of you we've been given a soul. Now up, up. It's time for breakfast."

Slipping out of the covers and off the sleeping sofa, she heard a faint humming. Another fine garment, this one the color of apricots, was being flown in on the wings of hummingbirds.

"So, it is you who brings me my clothes?"

"Yes, yes, and now we shall lead you to a breakfast fit for the gods, if you'll hurry. Come, come!"

After dressing, Psyche left her room and headed for the center of the palace. As she walked past, she glanced at the stairs that led to the west wing. There were no doors, no locks, but it was forbidden. Curious, but not enough to be defiant, she hurried past it and out onto the veranda.

She found an assortment of fruit, along with flaky bread layered with nuts and honey, and hard-boiled eggs for breakfast, lavishly laid out in one of the gardens.

As she had discovered over the past few weeks, each garden was more beautiful than the next. Some filled with exotic flowers, some with dense foliage, some dotted with statues, but this garden—the rose garden—was her favorite.

The shrubs and hedges surrounding it were well manicured, a vision of meticulous perfection. Within, a multitude of rosebushes climbed up high walls made of stone, twined through arched wooden trellises, and stood tall with thorny pride. Some rosebushes were in full bloom, while others were laden with buds; their petals still tightly wound, on the verge of gracing the world with their perfume.

She ate her breakfast, enjoying the breeze as it blew across her bare arms and the sun as it warmed her skin. She smiled fondly as her tiny companions flitted away to find some nectar of their own.

"I trust you slept well?"

Psyche gasped, her pulse jumping. *Syzygos*, she thought, and just as quickly, her lips lifted into a smile. "I slept soundly, thank you. What a surprise that you are here."

"I missed you while you slept. I thought I might walk with you before my beastly duties call me away. Fire and fury and all that." When he laughed, it was deep and soothing, like the purr of a great cat. "I can't stay long, but I shall come back when the sun sets, as always."

A warm hand enveloped hers, pulling her up from the table. "Come."

Psyche's heart began to race again, and she squeezed his hand to let him know she would follow.

"I gave your friends the gift of conscious thought, so they could keep you company. I hope they didn't frighten you."

"I'm getting used to voices on the wind around this place." She laughed, remembering the exchange in her bedchamber. "I would not have thought it possible, but they have much to say for such tiny creatures. The yellow one reminds me of my sister, Anika, a most serious

31

woman who is always lecturing. The orange one sounds like my mother."

"I am glad to hear they please you."

"They do, and I thank you for it."

"It's my pleasure to see you happy. Are you...?"

Psyche looked up at him, his glowing human shape barely visible in the light of day. "Am I happy here? I admit, in the beginning, I couldn't see how I truly would be, but with each day that has passed, each nightly debate and thought-provoking discussion that I very much look forward to, I find this place feeling more like my home. Better than home, even, for I would not be allowed to speak my mind there. But here it is my free will."

"And me? How do you feel about me? Do you still see me as your captor?"

Psyche shook her head. "No. Not a captor. Not a beast, either, but a friend."

She could not leave. She had no inkling how to get back to her father's kingdom, but the truth of the matter was she no longer cared to run. She had found something all her own here, in the way the wildflowers in the meadow seemed to grow just for her, and the brook in the forest bubbled to delight her and her alone.

How could she leave these things behind? These friends? And how could she leave him, with his tender words and gentle touch? She did not want to leave the one who, as it turned out, had the truest heart of all the men who had ever vied for her hand in marriage.

CHAPTER 5

THE WINGS OF the butterflies nestled within her hair fluttered—a living crown for his mortal queen—and the golden rays of sunlight made the chestnut streaks shine like copper. She was truly breathtaking. It was no wonder she'd been worshiped.

Weeks had passed, yet Eros's heart still ached knowing the woman walking in the gardens beside him had once thought him a treacherous beast. It was the farthest thing from the truth, but she'd had no way of knowing who—or what—he was other than what she'd been told by the Pythia.

Psyche was speaking of her family again, as she often did, and it made his wings feel as though they were made of lead. Perhaps he was a beast. He had set out with the cruelest of intentions not long ago, when his mother had sent him to put an end to the mortal who so brazenly dared to steal worship from her.

Smite her my son, for she has stolen what is rightfully mine.

Except, he had known the moment he'd laid eyes on Psyche she hadn't stolen a thing. It had

34

not been her doing, for men and women, old and young alike, had given their adoration freely, just as he did now.

She was a diamond among the rough, and that something so powerless and mundane as human seed could produce such exquisite beauty was a wonder.

Aphrodite had not seen it that way, however, and still did not, which was why he had asked Zephyrus to bring his gem here, a secret safe haven, away from the prying eyes, loose tongues, and wagging fingers of the gods.

A place his mother must never know existed.

The sunlight reflected in Psyche's amber eyes, bright golden flecks making them seem as though they held a universe of stars trapped inside glass. His divine heart beat faster than he believed possible at the thought that this was but the beginning of a lifetime gazing upon them. So long as she stayed in this palace, a place he had created for her—for them—they could be together.

But as good as his intentions were, guilt gnawed at his heart.

"I know that losing your family is difficult." *But it had been the only way...*

"I'm sorry," she said. "I know I speak of them endlessly but remembering eases the pain. I hope you understand."

She bent over to smell a rose and, with a wave of his hand, Eros made the half-opened bud bloom fully, the petals peeling apart as wide as his heart. He did understand, all too well, and it clawed at him that he was the reason she could no longer see her family. *She must seem dead and gone to everyone but me.*

"Did you do that for me?" She smiled as she inhaled the sweet fragrance.

"I do all things for you," he replied, commanding every bud on the bush to bloom into enormous red roses.

Psyche laughed, clasping her hands in delight. Soon after, worried fingers worked fingernails as she lowered her arms. "I wish you would show yourself to me..." She blushed deeply before going on. "So that I would know where to lay a kiss upon your cheek. I am not afraid anymore, if that is what you think."

At that moment, Eros wanted nothing more than for her to see him, for her to press a kiss onto his cheek, his lips, but the words his mother had once spoken stopped him from lifting his disguise.

Take heed this truth, Eros, my beloved son. Mortals are dangerous creatures, seeking fair faces over true hearts, for they are vainer than even the gods. Beware of their wretched and deceitful nature and remember, you are meant to pluck the heartstrings. It is not your heart to be played. Hear me now and listen well, never fall in love with a human for it will only bring you great suffering.

He cherished his mother, thinking her wise and wanting to please her. The goddess of love had given him life, after all, a purpose to be, so he had flown down from their sacred mountain that night and entered Psyche's room through the window. He had crept silently to where she had lain sleeping, intent on ending her life at the behest of Aphrodite.

It would have been easy to snatch the breath of the mortal beauty while she slept, but he could not bring himself to do it. Instead, his knees had gone weak at the sight of her, at the way her long, curling lashes rested upon her cheeks. His pulse had quickened as he'd leaned in close to caress a cheek, his heart filling with love and longing when his gaze fell to the conch shell pink of her lips.

He had never felt so much like a helpless mortal than in that moment. One look had been all it had taken for him to disobey his mother, deciding then to call upon the west wind to help him hide her.

And now, should his mother's words ring true, should he have made a mistake, and Psyche turned out to be the vain and deceitful creature his mother had warned she would be—though he could not fathom it, still, there was a part of him that could not be sure—Aphrodite would exact swift punishment by rescinding her affection.

The gods and goddesses of Mount Olympus were as spiteful as they were powerful, and, being a god himself, having seen the destruction caused by the squabbling grudges held between them firsthand, he knew just how spiteful. Aphrodite was no different. She would judge him unwise and ungrateful, having no qualms about punishing him severely for his trespass against her.

He shook the thought from his mind and continued walking through the gardens alongside Psyche, who was, again, speaking fondly of her family.

"I stood as maid of honor in the weddings of both my sisters. What grand celebrations they were."

Her words sounded wistful and happy, but her face was drawn.

"I know you can't see it, but love has not passed you by," said Eros, stopping to take her hands, passion to make her see him without her eyes—to *feel* him with her heart—igniting.

Perhaps Psyche could gaze upon his divine features one day, when he was sure she was not pretending, but today was not that day. Today would be the day he ensured she'd fall in love with his heart, not his face.

Eros pressed his lips to the back of one of her hands. "Talk about whatever you wish, butterfly, and I will listen."

He knew she could not see the sincerity in his eyes, but he knew by the tears that clung to the corners of hers, she could hear it.

"And you have listened, at great length." A breathy laugh lifted the sad lines of her face into a smile. "I'm surprised you have not torn me to pieces out of frustration, *syzygos*. You have been a true friend, and I am grateful for that, more than you know. I think, like the roses, that our friendship has blossomed into something else."

Eros pulled her into his arms, and she fell into them willingly. "I will challenge the sun a thousand times over. I will pull down the moon.

39

Say it is your wish and I will pluck the stars from the sky for you."

He felt her trembling, so he pulled her closer still, wrapping his wings around them both. She stayed in his embrace for what could have been hours, until finally, she pulled back to peer up at what she could see of him, which he knew was only a soft white glow.

It surprised him when her arms unlocked from around his waist, and her hands came around to slide over the ridges of his stomach, up over the expanse of his chest.

"Oh, my *syzygos*, are they green, your eyes? I imagine them as bright and tender as newly unfurled leaves." She explored until her fingers found his collarbone, and then she slowly dragged them over to his shoulder. "Your skin is as black as the night, isn't it?" Her thumb traced his jaw before she slid her fingers into his hair, and he found the sensation left him speechless. He was a hostage of his own powers: passion, desire, love, lust.

"And your hair, it is as dark and glossy as the wings of a raven. This is how I picture you, with shadowed beauty befitting of a ferocious bea—"

He was a god, not a beast, and he could not bear to hear the word fall from her lips, and so he pressed his mouth to hers. She yielded without hesitation, and he kissed her with an urgency he had not known could exist until that very moment.

The warning did not matter, and he did not care that he had deceived his mother, a goddess of immense power. This was right; it could not be wrong. It had been destiny for him to spare Psyche, he was certain. In her arms he was more than a god. He was time and space, night and day, chaos and order. He was everything and nothing without her.

Heart and soul, and by the hand of Fate, they were two halves made whole.

She gasped, breaking the kiss. "Feathers," she whispered, searching for his gaze with hers. How strange it must be for her to touch nothing but light and air, yet to be cradled by flesh and bone.

Eros blinked down at her, trying to make sense of what she'd said, until he realized her hands were gently stroking his wings.

"Your wings, they are made of feathers."

He smiled down at her, his butterfly, his precious diamond. What a sharp and beautiful mind his soul possessed, always working, always thinking.

His amusement rumbled in his throat. "My secret has been revealed. Did you not know? All hideous beasts have downy-soft wings. Why do you think we are capable of such terrible destruction? We are insane with embarrassment."

"A beast capable of humor. Who would have thought it possible?"

"Suppose they truly are feathers and not something I've conjured to keep you at ease. Would that ruin the image of me in your mind's eye?"

She laughed, a melodious sound that made him want to do all he promised and more. "No, I don't think anything could change my image of you, but it does prove one thing. I do not need to see your face to know your heart."

CHAPTER 6

IF PSYCHE DID not stop drinking the delicious honeyed wine now, she would never make it back to her room on her own two feet.

Her lips curled into a mischievous grin as she took another sip.

For months their dinner had been laid out by the same invisible hands, then cleared away after they had finished. She was accustomed to objects floating in mid-air as her every need was anticipated and mysteriously attended to, sometimes even before she knew she needed it.

Her *syzygos* had not lied—she did not want for anything. Yet, there was one thing she did long for and had not received.

She fixed a half-lidded gaze on the glowing light at the head of the table, conjuring her image of him. It spurred her mouth to open. "You accepted me as your bride, but we have spoken no marriage vows. Why is that?"

"Because you are here with me, cheeks ruddy from sweet wine, and that is all the promise I need."

"We live as husband and wife, yet we do not share the same bed. Does my mortal flesh repulse you?" Psyche's cheeks grew warm, nervous at what her *syzygos* might say. She was a mortal, after all, and he was... not.

"Quite the opposite. I find you to be the most alluring creature I've ever laid eyes upon."

She blew out a sigh before a sudden streak of defiance lifted her chin. "Then why have you not come to me?"

"I have never been with a mortal before. What if I hurt you?"

"Hurt me?" She had not thought of that.

"Power unimaginable courses through my veins, Psyche. What if I get carried away and crush the breath from your lungs? I could never forgive myself. I love you too much."

"Then it is true?" she said, pushing up from her chair. "There is love between us." She held onto the table for balance as she put one foot in front of the other, equally unsteady and bold in her drunkenness. She only meant to move to another chair, so she could sit closer to him, but she suddenly found herself standing before him, swaying on shaky legs.

"I love you like I have loved no other," he said, also rising. "If it is vows you want, I fear I may be powerless to deny you."

He pulled her to him, wrapping one arm around her head, the other across her back and shoulders. He smelled soft like roses, sweet like summer grass, like warm sun-kissed skin and wind-swept hair. All the things she loved, and she melted into his embrace.

"And the pleasures known to husband and wife?" she murmured into his chest.

He sighed. "Psyche."

"I'm sorry," she said, pressing closer. "I thought this place would be enough, but it is lonely without you. I long to share everything with you, even my body."

They stood in silence as he stroked the back of her head. After what seemed like an eternity, he spoke. "Then I say it now, the gods as my witnesses, I pledge my love and honor to you from this day forward. You are mine and I am yours, heart and soul."

She could tell by the way the air shifted that he had leaned back to appraise her reaction. The weight of his hands rested at the back of her neck as he traced the line of her jaw with his thumbs.

She smiled wide, her heart near to bursting. "And I to you. I vow to love and honor you for the rest of my days, heart and soul."

The glowing outline pulsed, and when it stretched and grew like a hatchling breaking free of its shell, she knew he had spread his wings. Eddies of air swirled across her skin as his wings unfurled, the sound like crisp linen snapping in the wind.

"Our vows have been spoken," he said, soft and low. "Let us seal them with a kiss, and never break trust."

Psyche tilted her head upward, and when his lips touched hers something indefinable sparked both fire and ice through her veins. It was magic, she knew instantly. Whether the power belonged to him or had come from somewhere deep within the universe, it did not matter. The pact they had made between them was binding.

Her hands rested on his chest, but when he deepened the kiss, she slid them around his neck. She continued to revel in the warmth of his glow until he lifted her feet out from under her.

She floated, cradled in light, strong arms around her back and behind her knees. The sensation made her dizzy when she began to float out of the dining room.

Psyche trembled in his arms, for she knew where he was taking her. And she wanted him to, so they could create another sort of magic.

He carried her through the hall to the east wing and to the door of her bedchamber, but he did not go inside. Instead, she felt a tender kiss on her forehead. He was waiting for permission, and so she caressed his jaw before guiding his lips to her mouth to give him the answer.

When their mouths finally parted, he set her down, and she pulled him under the archway. The light within was dim, the air chilled, and when she began to prepare an oil lamp, he came to stand behind her, reaching around to gently still her hands. All light, including that which veiled him, vanished, and she stood in complete darkness, unable to see.

Oh, but she could feel.

His hands trailed up her arms. She felt him push aside her hair and shivered when he planted a kiss on her neck. His very human arousal pressed into her back, and a sharp inhale raised her chest when he reached both hands around to cup her breasts, peaked beneath the silky fabric. His appreciative exhale caused warmth to pool between her legs.

"You're shivering." His breath tickled her ear. "Are you cold... or frightened?"

"Yes... no. I think cold, perhaps."

"You will be warm soon enough."

Before she could reply, nimble fingers lifted the hem of her dress. They slid their way up her calves and along her thighs, the silk bunching in the small of her back when he gripped both of her hips. She arched into him, making contact with a pair of strong, naked thighs.

He leaned into her in return, splaying a hand across her belly as the other roamed over the plain of her thigh, moving in slow, agonizing circles. She gasped when it reached its final destination.

No man had ever touched Psyche in that way before, let alone a creature of such raw power. His fingertips vibrated as they stroked her most sensitive skin. The sensation was overwhelming, and when her knees began to give out, he lifted her once again, carrying her to the bed.

He placed her down gently, his mouth never leaving hers, before lying next to her. She nestled into his warmth as he caressed her back. She felt his need again, thick and heavy between them, and before long, the exquisite pressure built within her once more. When she could stand it no longer, she tugged at her dress, relieving her body of it so that she could press her skin to his.

It was smooth and hot, his skin, and he pulled her closer, kissing her with a growing urgency that made her own skin flush. When he shifted on top of her, she twined a leg around his thigh. Her fingertips explored the place where feathered wing met muscled back, and she was in awe of each hard ridge and soft curve. They were half folded, his wings, stretching outward a little more whenever she stroked them. She smiled as she returned his reverent kisses, half expecting him to purr like a feline.

"Now, my love," she whispered, slick with her own desire. She could not live a single second longer without being one with him.

When he entered her, she cried out, lost in the feeling of completeness she'd found. When she arched her hips to meet his, the tears clinging to the corners of her eyes swelled. And as she soared on the wings of love to the highest heights of passion, they fell.

CHAPTER 7

EROS GRAZED HIS fingertips down the back of Psyche's arm. She lay nestled against his chest, her eyes moving beneath her lids as she slept. He longed to wake her, to make love again, but he decided to watch her dream instead.

How many times had he seen her this way? Not enough, and he could not fathom ever tiring of the sight. When Psyche stirred, issuing the softest of sighs from her lips before turning over, Eros pulled her to him, curling his body around hers and covering them both with his wings.

He could not remember feeling so content as he reveled in the rhythm of her breathing. After a long while, his eyes began to grow heavy, and so he kissed the back of her head before slowly untangling himself from her limbs. It was time to retire to the west wing, to the safety of his room. Should he fall asleep and the illusion that veiled him slip...

And what if she awoke to discover the truth?

He dared not think of it, of what would happen if his magic faltered while he slept. For it was the greatest irony of all that, as a god, he could wield such great power over mortals, influencing their affections—their deepest desires—toward one another, yet still fall prey to basic human trappings like thirst, hunger, and the need to rest.

He floated from her room, his wings carrying him down the hall and through the grand foyer without a sound. By the time he entered his own chambers, his heart weighed heavy with sorrow and regret. Not that he'd spirited her away from the mortal world, he would do that a thousand times over, but that he'd kept his true identity from her, letting her believe he was a hideous monster.

At first, the deception had been to protect her. Eros could not be sure she wouldn't burn away like Semele when she'd demanded to gaze upon Zeus in all his divine glory. The poor mortal woman, easily tricked by Zeus's jealous wife, Hera, had disintegrated into a pile of ashes on the spot.

But Zeus and Hera were the most powerful of all the gods and goddesses, and when Eros realized Semele's demise had been more from Hera's rage than anything, veiling himself from Psyche hadn't been to avoid her untimely death, but a way to protect her from another jealous goddess. His mother.

And, beyond that, a test to see if Psyche's mortal heart was as vain as Aphrodite had said it would be. To his pure delight, and utter relief, it had turned out she was not.

Eros laid his head on a pillow, comforted by the thought as he wrapped his wings around his shoulders. The prophecy, although he had been irritated at being interpreted as a winged serpent, had proven to be the least of his woes. Little had he known the assurance the love he gave would be returned freely and truly— assurance that his heart would not be destroyed by the heat of human passion or the flames of mortal lust—would come with a price. Guilt.

Eros threw open the curtains surrounding his bed, the golden rays of sunrise greeting him with brilliant shades of orange and gold. He fanned his wings and stretched, shaking away the last remnants of slumber.

He had just climbed onto the sill of the open window, ready to take flight and conduct his business for the day, when a trio of small voices beckoned to him.

"Sire, wait!" The butterflies danced in circles, each fluttering around and bouncing off the other as they moved closer. "May we have a word?"

"Of course," said Eros, stepping down from the ledge. "What is it, friends?"

"It is the lady, sire. We've come to tell you how she longs to see her family. Forgive us, but she would never let it be known, for she loves you and does not want to provoke your anger, but we see how she weeps in the gardens during the day, drying her eyes before you arrive in the evening."

Eros crossed the room, lowering onto his bed to consider what the tiny messengers had relayed. With every beat, his heart grew heavier, until he dropped his head into his hands. "I should have known it would not be enough."

Almost a full year she had endured her loneliness, for him.

Perhaps her sisters could visit, just once. He would ask Mnemosyne to clear away all memory of how they'd arrived, and all they had seen and heard, so they would only take with them when they left closure and the peace of mind their sister was in a better place.

Surely there would be no stories for his mother to catch wind of if they did not remember.

I owe her this, he thought as he stood, his resolve to deny her from seeing her family again crumbling. *For believing me though I have lied.* Decision made, he climbed onto the sill again and dove headlong into the sky.

The sun slipped beneath the horizon just as Eros took a sip of the rose-gold liquid in his cup. But the surge of vitality the nectar of the gods gave him could not compare to the feeling that raced through his veins when he heard Psyche's breathless laughter.

"When?" She pushed away from the dinner table, flushed from her excitement. "How soon?"

He smiled as he watched her twirl in circles alongside the butterflies. It brought him almost as much pleasure as striking his golden arrows into the hearts of man.

"Will you meet them?" asked Psyche, feeling about the chair in which he sat before she settled onto his lap.

He slid one arm around her waist, resting the other on the silk draped over her thighs. "As soon as you wish, my love. And, no, I think

I shall be away while they are here. My presence will only be a distraction, and I do not wish to compromise your reunion."

"Where shall I say you have gone?" She caught her bottom lip between her teeth. "*What* should I tell them you are?"

"Tell them I am your *syzygos*, and that I am merely away on diplomatic business but do hope they will enjoy the hospitality I have extended. I will bestow your tiny, winged friends with mortal shells. I'm sure floating plates and speaking insects would be a terrible shock to your sisters."

Psyche giggled.

"But Psyche," continued Eros in a more serious tone. "You must give me your word you will not tell them about our life here."

It was a grave risk, letting her see them. Even if Mnemosyne altered their memories, there was no guarantee they would fully forget. Human minds had a way of puzzling out the trickery of gods.

But she was so happy, and he could deny her nothing. And then there was the matter of his guilt.

"So, they must not know you are a..." She hesitated, her brows furrowing as she tried to think of the right words to say. "Being of immense power?"

"Yes, and you must offer them as little detail as possible."

"Why?"

"For reasons I cannot explain but believe me when I say that bringing your sisters here is of great sacrifice. If they find out the half of it..." He didn't want to put the fear of the gods in her, but the thought of losing her was too great. "You could anger Aphrodite again. And if that happens, I would be forced to—"

"I promise." She said before he could finish.

Eros exhaled, relieved she didn't press the issue further. He had no idea what he would do if they were discovered. "Good. Then it's settled. Let's enjoy our dinner."

"But what if I should like to reward you justly for your sacrifice now?" Her voice was husky with desire, and she found his mouth easily. She kissed him, pulling back to smile seductively when she tasted the nectar on his lips. Eros knew how ambrosia affected mortals, and he smiled back, looking forward to what would follow.

Their lovemaking had been vigorous, and now they lay in each other's arms, finally spent.

Eros brushed the hair from Psyche's damp forehead, letting his fingers comb through the long strands.

"Where do you go at night, after I fall asleep?" she asked.

"To my lair." He could not resist the jest. When the silence between them grew, he caressed her hip. "You know where I go. To my own room in the west wing."

"Why?" she murmured, on the verge of falling asleep.

"Trust me when I say it must be this way," he whispered, tracing the contours of her face. "And I will always wait until you are asleep and dreaming before leaving your bed."

Her soft snores curled his lips. She was so utterly mortal, and he was so irrevocably in love. He would do anything to make her happy.

His smile faded, a new and sudden thought, one that rivaled keeping his true identity hidden, stealing it from his face like a brazen thief. Her beautiful, inquisitive soul was human, and his immortal. How long would they have together, even if he did keep up his façade?

He knew the answer immediately. If they were to be together forever, he must go behind his mother's back and take the matter directly to Zeus. There was no other way, for the king of the gods was the only one powerful enough to grant immortality.

A new question formed in his mind. What if it was all for naught? If Psyche did not wish to live for eternity, then the strings of his heart had indeed been played.

CHAPTER 8

PSYCHE HUMMED ABSENTLY, admiring the wildflowers in the meadow as she waited for her sisters to arrive. After a while, she lay in the grass, peering up at the sky to watch the clouds roll by. As most days, the sun was bright and the wind gentle and warm. A rustling in the distance caught her attention and she quickly sat up. A small smile touched her lips when she discovered the white doe approaching her.

The doe bent her head and nudged Psyche's shoulder. She reached up and stroked the deer's long neck lovingly. The wildlife around the palace had become accustomed to her presence, and often times even seeking her out. She returned their fondness in kind.

She lay back once more, and the doe moved on to nibble a patch of clover nearby. A bee buzzed from one flower to the next, and it wasn't long before Psyche's mind wandered off to the morning's events, starting with being gently shaken awake by a young maid, breathing and visible as any human.

"Oh!" Psyche had exclaimed, sitting up in her bed. "How lovely you are."

The girl had large, vivid blue eyes—just like her wings had been—and the faintest blush of pink tinting her cheeks. "Thank you, my lady!"

"What is your name?" Psyche had tilted her head, waiting patiently for the girl to answer.

"I... I don't think I have a name." The girl had paused thoughtfully. "Will you give me one?"

Psyche had laughed then, delighted by the girl's sweet nature. "Of course. How about Morpho? Do you like that name?"

The young maid had nodded her head, pleased.

Just then an older woman had entered the room carrying Psyche's clothes. "Ah, she's awake! Come, come, you have a very big day. Your sisters will be arriving soon."

Psyche had giggled, instantly knowing which of the butterflies the older woman had been. "You must be the orange butterfly, the one that reminds me of my mother. May I call you Danaus?"

"Of course, of course! I am honored to be given such a beautiful name by you, my lady."

Psyche had thrown off the blankets and climbed out of bed by this time, pulling first

Morpho and then Danaus into a hug. "My beloved friends, I am most pleased to be able to embrace you, but where is the third? The yellow one?"

An impatient scoff had come from just beyond the chamber door, and soon after a middle-aged woman, tall and gaunt, with yellow hair and rather severe features, much like her temperament, had entered the room.

"There you are!" Psyche had cried, delighted at having the last of her butterfly companions in the flesh before her.

"So I am. Now, hurry, all of you. There is no time to dawdle."

"Papilio," Psyche had said.

"Pardon?" The yellow-haired maid had stopped what she was doing to stand in the center of the room and blink at Psyche.

"Your name. She has given you your name. Mine is Morpho." The young maid had twirled in circle as she'd said it.

"Yes, yes, and mine is Danaus."

Papilio had tried to hide her delighted smile by rushing over to pick up the pile of blankets on the floor. "Very well," she had said, smoothing them across the bed in a very precise and methodical manner. "If I must have a name, I suppose Papilio is suitable enough."

After that, Morpho had helped Psyche bathe and dress. Danaus had seen to her breakfast, and Papilio had grumbled at how slowly she had done this or that. Now she sat in the meadow, humming a sweet melody and waiting.

The sound of a snapping twig sent the doe galloping away, and Psyche sprang up from her spot, anxious and hopeful, just as two figures emerged from the trees.

"Psyche!" called out the younger of the two women.

"Anika!" Psyche broke into a run, lifting the bottom of her silk peplos so that she could get to her sisters faster. "Phyllis!"

When she reached them, Psyche gathered them to her, hooking an arm around each of them and squeezing until all three were laughing breathlessly.

"It is true, then," said Phyllis, pulling back to hold Psyche by the shoulders and examine her more closely. "Our little sister is alive and well." She smiled with lips the same shape as Psyche's, only thinner.

"*Very* well, it seems." Anika nodded with arched brows toward the gleaming palace towering in the distance.

"I'm so happy to see you both," replied Psyche, ignoring Anika's remark. What did the size of her home matter when they had been apart for so long? "I've missed you both so much. Come! It is after noon. You must be famished."

They began walking toward the palace, and had not taken more than a few steps when Anika asked, "But tell us, sister, for we are most curious to know, what happened up on the mountain?"

"Why, as you can see, dear sister, a marriage!" Psyche tried to keep the ire out of her voice. She did not know how long her sisters would be allowed to stay. This should be a joyous reunion, free of such trivial details.

"Anika. Let us enjoy this happy moment. There will be a more appropriate time for questions." Phyllis glanced at Psyche. "And answers."

No more inquiries of Psyche's night on the mountain came as they walked through the meadow, but of Anika's husband's newest business venture, and what luxuries the profits afforded her. Phyllis's news of a second pregnancy was most welcome, and by the time they reached the steps of the palace, Psyche was feeling much happier, for she cherished their talk of life back home.

The doors opened as the women ascended the stairs to the porch. When they reached the entrance, Danaus greeted them.

"Welcome, welcome." She swept her arm wide, an invitation for them to come in. Morpho and Papilio smiled warmly, looking on from behind Danaus.

"Thank you, Danaus," said Psyche as they stepped into the foyer. "These are my sisters, Anika and Phyllis."

Anika's mouth dropped open, her head swiveling from one side to the other as she took in the richness of the palace. The marbled floors, the golden fixtures, the precious gems inlaid beneath their feet. Even Phyllis's eyes grew wide.

"Let's eat, shall we? Danaus, is the midday meal ready?

"Of course, my lady. Please follow me."

Danaus led the way, Morpho and Papilio trailing after Psyche and her sisters. A table on the terrace held an abundance of food. Heaped high on trays, it was more than three women could possibly finish. When each had been seated, the maids poured the sweet red wine.

Anika spoke as she filled her plate from the many platters before her. "We have waited long enough. It is time for answers. Speak plain, sister, for the oracle said that you would die at the hands of a winged beast, yet you live, and like a queen besides, in lavishness the likes of which I have never seen. Tell us, from what kingdom does your *syzygos* inherit his riches?"

Anika had always been preoccupied with wealth and status. It appeared nothing had changed. It irritated Psyche to no end, driving her last thread of patience to snap and causing her to lash out like a petulant child.

"He has not told it to me, but my guess is Hades. Why, that is where he is now, dear sister, counting the coins tithed by the unfortunate souls whom Charon has ferried across the River Styx."

The clattering of silver made all three women jump, and Psyche turned in time to see a set of bowls wobbling at Morpho's feet. Their eyes met, and a frightened look flashed across the girl's face before she took a few unsteady steps backward. Then, suddenly spinning on her heels, she darted forward, then side-to-side. She fluttered about like this—like the butterfly she was—for several minutes before Papilio rushed in to stop her.

"Oh, for the love of the gods. Come here, Morpho." Papilio gave Psyche a look of reproach before ushering the still flailing girl from the dining room.

Psyche swallowed, guilt and remorse swelling her throat.

"Is the girl simple?" Anika plucked an olive from the tray in front of her.

"No. Only easily overwhelmed."

Anika's gaze flicked toward Phyllis before settling on Psyche. "Your maids, they are strange, with too-blue eyes, orange-tinted skin and hair the color of a canary. Are they from the Underworld, too?"

Psyche couldn't tell if Anika was only teasing or truly suspicious, but her refusal to relish their time together filled Psyche with an equal measure of hurt and disappointment.

"Does it matter?" Psyche looked at the food on the table pointedly. "It seems they have served you just as well."

"It does not matter from where they come." Phyllis placed a protective hand over the slight swell of her belly. Her voice was sympathetic, for she knew just as well as Psyche did how relentless Anika could be, especially when jealous. "Anika, leave our little sister to her secrets."

Psyche lifted her chin, trying to exude calm even as her stomach twisted itself into knots. It was the truth; she *was* keeping secrets. She just wasn't privy to what they were, and it made her cheeks burn. Her jaw clenched tight, for she was suddenly angry with her husband for keeping her in the dark.

CHAPTER 9

The air grew still, heavy with truths Psyche could not ignore. She'd never set eyes upon the face of her *syzygos*, and his reasons why had been enough. Until Anika's needling gave her pause.

Psyche had chosen to believe with her heart in place of her eyes. Given everything that had transpired, there hadn't seemed a reason not to. But now, with her sister's incessant questions and dogged determination to snatch away the sureness of her heart, she thought that perhaps she might have been a fool.

But wasn't that just like Anika? Undermining others' happiness because the need to have what others had—and more—was insatiable?

"Let us abandon this talk of beasts," said Psyche, suddenly angry, a twinge of petulance in her voice. She would not fall prey to her sister's insecurities. The woman did not have to believe that one could fall in love with invisible beings, but the least she could do was not try to diminish Psyche's happiness. "Come, I will show you around."

A tour might exacerbate Anika's jealousy, encouraging her mouth to keep moving, but Psyche could no longer tolerate her sister's contrivances. Psyche's heart had been laden with doubt earlier, but now it was weighed down with annoyance. Phyllis's reluctance to curb Anika's antics added to the disappointment, causing Psyche to grow weary of their visit, and anxious for it to end.

She led her sisters through the sprawling palace in silence, waiting patiently when Phyllis stopped to admire one of several larger-than-life marble statues of Aphrodite and her son Eros that lined the long hallway.

Phyllis placed a hand on her stomach, her fingers splayed protectively. "Why so many likenesses of Aphrodite?"

"All the Olympians have a place in our home," Psyche remarked simply. She had never thought it strange before and searched for some reason why it should make her sister wary.

Phyllis and Anika exchanged a look.

"Aphrodite is the goddess of love, something of which you have been deprived," continued Phyllis. "Do you not see the irony?"

"I am not deprived of love," replied Psyche, intending to explain.

But what could she say? That she gave and received love from a glowing light that somehow had the weight of flesh and solidness of bone? Surely, they would think her delusional.

"Is it your eyes that fail you?" said Anika, tilting her head. "Or is it your wits? It is clear there was more to the prophecy. It was foretold that only a beast would take you as a wife. This part of the prophecy has come to pass. The oracle said nothing about your death. The gods are as dangerous and cruel as they are kind and benevolent. When angered, they do not forget. Can't you see? The man you call husband is a beast in disguise, exacting Aphrodite's punishment even now. What greater revenge for an angered goddess than for a mortal who has wronged her to suffer torment unwittingly?"

Shrewd Anika's bitter words found the cracks in Psyche's stoic façade, prying them open wider. The certainty her husband was not deceiving her began to trickle out of her but Psyche quickly thrust anger into the fissures, stopping them from giving way before her calm demeanor crumbled completely.

"For the last time, he is not a beast," snapped Psyche. He had his reasons, and she had promised to accept them. "He is tending to his business, as I have told you. Now, can you find it within to stop this meddling and be happy for me? I am alive and well. I am simply not privy to his dealings, as you are not with your husband. As all wives are not. My husband is not a monster. He is a kind and gentle soul who treats me well."

"What kind of *man* does not postpone his work so that he may greet his wife's family into his home? Why is he not here, sister? Has he something to hide? Wild, bulging eyes and a wicked forked tongue, perhaps?"

You must offer as little detail as possible.

Psyche's mouth bobbed open and shut. She wanted to scream how wrong they were, but her lips refused to form the answers to her sister's questions.

"What is his business? Is he a merchant? A tradesman? What type of dealings garners this much glittering wealth?" Anika swept her arms wide. "The size alone is staggering, this place that sits uncharted and unknown to men. Your halfwit sputtering instead of answers speaks for itself."

Phyllis tried to soften the sharp edge of Anika's tone. "We are frightened for you, sister, that is all. It seems that you are still a lamb on the altar perpetually awaiting sacrifice. That is no way to live. Anika speaks the truth. The unearthly feel of this place, the unnaturalness of its servants... Leave with us and come home."

You could anger Aphrodite again. And if that happens, I would be forced to—

The memory of her lover's words echoed in Psyche's head. The idea that she was still paying for her trespass, living a one-sided love in exile for the rest of her life made the hairs at the back of her neck rise. Perhaps this was Aphrodite's cruel revenge: her torment cleverly disguised as true love.

There seemed scarcely enough air to fill Psyche's lungs. A worm of doubt wriggled uncomfortably in her belly. Was her husband bound by duty to keep her here, so that Aphrodite could take pleasure from Psyche's ignorance for the rest of her days? The gods did so love trickery, especially when accompanied with irony. As much as she didn't want to believe their vows had been part of an elaborate ruse, one she had been too daft to see through, the possibility seemed plausible.

If only she could see his face, look into his eyes, then she might know the truth of it.

"How do we even get back? I have no memory of how we came to be in the woods surrounding this palace." Anika turned toward Phyllis, raising her eyebrows in question. "Do you?"

Phyllis's brows crumpled before her gaze turned toward Psyche. "I cannot recall, which is all the more reason we must leave at once."

Psyche could scarcely think, her thoughts a jumbled mess. Her head spun as she tried to think of something to say that would calm her sisters.

Believe me when I say that bringing your sisters here is of great sacrifice.

Their visit had indeed been a risk. She could see that now.

Anika folded her arms, nodding her head knowingly. "I see. You do not wish to give up this luxury, but rather have your family in constant turmoil and worry. We see now that you cannot be reasoned with. Stay here, then, but know that we tried to save you, Psyche."

Anika was right; her sisters must leave the palace as quickly as possible. But she would stay. There were questions that needed answers. If her husband refused to answer them, then she would wait, and when the time was right, she would quietly slip into the west wing and learn the truth with her own eyes.

Psyche lifted her gaze to the heavens, closing her eyes before invoking a god she hoped would listen this time. "I call upon you now, oh mighty Zephyrus."

She could only imagine the looks of terror on her sister's faces as a warm wind began to swirl throughout the palace, but she could not open her eyes now. "Carry my sisters from here with your gentle hands."

For a moment, she thought Zephyrus would hear her prayer but not grant her request, but a series of whistling gusts soon allayed her fear. Warm air rushed through her hair, making it rise and whip like the tentacles of a kraken. Yet, her still shut lids squeezed tighter, for there was one more god she needed to ask a favor.

"Mnemosyne, mother of muses, goddess of memory, let them forget what they have seen." Lids still closed Psyche slowly sank to her knees before lowering her chest to the ground. She knew her sisters would not be there when she opened her eyes. When she uttered the rest of her prayer, the words tasted like ash in her mouth. "Let them forget they ever had a sister at all."

CHAPTER 10

EROS SIGHED AT the way candlelight and shadow played upon the soft waves of Psyche's hair. Although his time spent on Olympus had been filled with feasting and gossiping over the latest affairs of Zeus, three days away from his mortal queen had seemed like an eternity, and he was happy to be with her once more.

But there had been a strange uneasiness between them since his return.

Her silence had grown heavier throughout the day, pressing her lips into a thin line with each minute that passed, until he could ignore the weight of it no longer.

"You've barely spoken a word since I've returned, my love." He lifted a goblet of rose-gold nectar to his lips, hoping the sip of ambrosia would relieve him of the strange and foreign swirling in his belly. "Was the reunion not a joyous occasion?"

"It was joyous enough," she murmured before returning to rearranging the folds of her gown, as if the task was of the utmost importance.

Eros had grown fond of her pensive moods and constant ruminations, finding them curious and endearing, but when the moments passed and no further explanation came, the smile that had been playing at the corners of his mouth dropped into a frown.

"Come now, wife, tell me what is vexing you."

She finally looked at him, fixing her gaze on his glowing aura with a furrowed brow. When she spoke again, her words were soft, but there was no mistaking the hard edge beneath them. "You knew the way of it. It was ill conceived for them to come. They had many questions."

Concern tugged at him, tightening his chest, and he rose to draw closer. She lifted a hand, indicating he should abandon his advance. He stilled, waiting for what he knew would come next, and bracing himself for what would follow.

"What questions did they ask?"

"Questions of your identity. Where you acquired these riches and how." Psyche gestured toward the golden fixtures and gleaming marble. "They thought me a liar—and worse, a gullible fool—when I could not give them answers."

"Why on Earth would they call you a fool?"

76

"Don't you see? That is the question... *Are* we on Earth? They could not remember by which route they had traveled, and I could not tell them, though I knew they had been carried to this place by the hand of Zephyrus, as I had been. They are keen, my sisters, and I was forced to *lie*."

The pounding of Eros's heart filled his ears, nearly drowning out her voice. As always, she spoke the truth. He had indeed asked her to lie by omission.

"They claim the prophecy has not fully come to pass," she continued, "that I am still being punished by the gods. That Aphrodite smiles when she looks down upon me, satisfied in her revenge that I have fallen in love with a beast who deceives me at her behest. What evidence could I give them to prove otherwise?"

"The unknown frightens man," said Eros through a clenched jaw. She had agreed to keep what details she knew a secret, so that she could reunite with her sisters. He had thought she had understood the risk, and the sacrifice that would need to accompany it. So why was she now accusing him of *forcing* her to lie?

The thought caused the petulance all gods were capable of, even the god of love, to careen toward the surface. It raked at his patience along the way, but Eros kept harsh words from a sharp tongue at bay.

Psyche did not show the same restraint, and her voice rose, trembling with anger with each question she asked. "No truer words spoken, husband. So why, then, have you kept yourself hidden from me? Are you truly a beast? And will you discard me once Aphrodite has had her fill? Once she tires of my suffering, what will you do with me then?"

Eros closed his eyes as he drew in a calming breath. When he opened them, he spoke the only truth he could. "I will love you for all eternity, no matter what poison Aphrodite's jealousy rains down upon us. Even after you are dead and gone, I will still love you."

Psyche sprang from the chair in which she'd been sitting. "Then you admit it! You are a beast, under persuasion and sworn to punish me by using the true love I have dreamt of possessing my entire life against me. I will die, then, and I will go to my grave having been an utter fool."

The tears streaming down her cheeks drained all annoyance from him, leaving the space to quickly fill with pity and remorse. How had he thought keeping her here would be enough? Her inquisitive human nature, her need to think and analyze and *know,* had once been a drawing force, but now it threatened to tear them apart. He should have known keeping the truth hidden from her would lead to this.

Perhaps he had known all along, but her beauty had blinded him; lit the flame of his desire and burned away every thought of consequence the moment he'd laid eyes on her. In an instant, that which he had carelessly bestowed upon others had been plunged deep into his own heart, and his love for Psyche had been swift and irrevocable.

Eros shook his head even though he knew Psyche could not see him. Despite his mother's warning, he could not—would not—go back to a life without her. "No, Psyche. I love you of my own free will. I have not been persuaded, nor have I sworn to punish you. But I cannot explain my actions, and you must trust me that it's for your own good."

Color rose into her cheeks, quick as lightning. "Do not tell me what is for my own good, for I have sacrificed much. I have given myself over to prophecy *willingly,* so that I may appease the wrath of an unforgiving goddess. Despite my lot, I have come to believe impossible things. That gods and monsters exist as surely as mortals live and breathe. That divine power and prophecy are real and absolute. I made a promise to give up life as I knew in exchange for a marriage to someone— some *thing*—I knew not. To fulfill the prophecy, nay, the *curse* that had been cast upon me and save my family from the same fate. I've kept my end of the bargain, husband. What have you done?"

Eros could not stop his fists from balling; an involuntary reaction to the pain her words had inflicted. "You call our marriage a *bargain?*"

An unfathomable hurt he had never experienced before pierced through his chest, and his wings unfurled, snapping open with force.

"You have hidden things from me!" Psyche was yelling now, her eyes wild and trained on him—his light, heating like a flame—as he hovered high above her. "What is it you do not want your wife to know, husband? The depths of your deception? If you love me as you say you do, then *show me your face.*"

"Enough!" bellowed Eros, his anger breaking free of restraint. "I will have no more of this. Does sparing your life mean nothing? Have you no gratitude for all I have given you, for the kindness I have shown you? For the love we share? I've told you all I can and that must be enough. *Your life depends on it.*"

At that, Psyche dropped her face into her hands and wept. Whether she had succumbed to the throes of her anger or she felt reproached by his words, Eros could not say. A part of him longed to wrap his arms around her, stroke her sweet head and whisper words of comfort into her ear. Yet, another part seethed with anger at her dogged determination and inability to let the matter go.

"I love you with all of my heart, Psyche," he said, feet touching the ground once more. Had he ever felt so weary as he did at that moment? "It is true that I am not a man, but I am no beast. Believe me when I say it pains me your questions must go unanswered."

Conscience heavy, Eros sighed as he turned from his love and walked toward the west wing.

CHAPTER 11

PSYCHE LAY AWAKE in her bed, the events of
the evening turning over endlessly in her mind.
She had been able to do nothing else since
they'd quarreled.

Her attendants had tried to console her
when she fled from the dining room, but it had
been no use, and she had sent them away once
she'd reached her bedchamber. It comforted
her to know one of them would stay close,
somewhere outside the door just in case she'd
needed them, but it hadn't been enough to dry
her tears.

The embers inside the brazier glowed, and
only a small flame flickered from deep within
the hearth. The palace was always comfortable,
never unbearably cold, but Psyche shivered
despite being nestled under thick bed covers.

You call our marriage a bargain?

Remembering the hurt in her husband's
voice made her wince. She had accused him of
evil things, and without grace. She had been
uncivilized in her manner, screaming and
carrying on, and she couldn't help but wonder
if she were the beast.

Unable to remain still, Psyche pushed off the covers. She lit the oil lamp at her bedside table and surveyed the rolls of stacked papyrus. If sleep eluded her, perhaps reading would help clear her thoughts and occupy her mind. At least until morning, when she would make amends. Not for speaking the truth, but for the venom that had made her words poisonous.

Psyche made her selection, then pulled a covering from her bed and dragged it toward one of the chairs sitting in front of the hearth. Once settled, she began to unroll the text, but quickly found herself staring into the dying fire.

Does sparing your life mean nothing?

Wood and flames and stone swirled into a watery blur before her eyes. The urge to go to him now, and not wait until morning, nearly drew her to her feet, but the order to never set foot in the west wing stayed her.

Surely, he was as heartsick and forlorn from the argument as she. He would make an exception, wouldn't he?

Psyche stood, wrapping the expanse of woven wool over her gauzy shift, and retrieved the oil lamp. She needed to tell him that she did appreciate all that he had done, no matter how ungrateful his impression of her at the moment.

The heavy wooden and wrought iron door creaked, although, blessedly, not loudly enough to disturb Danaus, who had fallen asleep in a most uncomfortable looking chair across from the door of her bedchamber. Psyche smiled at her fondly, holding her breath when the old woman stirred in her sleep. When Danaus finally settled, Psyche quickly padded past her and down the hall.

The light from the oil lamp danced around her, illuminating the stone floor and walls only a few steps ahead. Whether her husband was a beast or something else, it was plain he was capable of grace and kindness and love. She must go to him, unburdening her heavy heart by telling him so, no matter the consequences.

Psyche passed through the great arch that led into the west wing. The air hummed with a power that raised the fine hair on her arms. Her pulse quickened, and her chest heaved with the pace of it, yet the sorrow and regret clawing at her conscience urged her to continue.

There was a set of winding stairs at the end of the corridor, and she climbed them carefully, taking each step one-by-one. When she reached the top, she entered a small ante chamber.

The presence of a tall figure looming in the corner stopped her in her tracks. Had he anticipated she would come? Had he been waiting for her?

Psyche stepped closer, lifting the lamp high, a questioning murmur falling from her lips. *"Syzygos?"*

Psyche nearly dropped the light when she discovered what stood before her—a great golden bow, elegantly curved and standing several feet high.

She marveled at how it floated above the ground in front of her, held there by an unseen magical force. The light danced over its gilded surface as she moved the lamp higher in an attempt to see the top.

Whether it was for hunting or for war, bows were ever only used for one thing. Killing. But how could a thing of such delicate beauty be a weapon?

Psyche shook the thought from her mind as she moved toward the massive set of doors. Once again, she held out the lamp, this time to inspect their intricately carved surfaces. She discovered they were not inlaid, nor gilded, but made of solid gold, with engraved scenes of

unsuspecting victims shot through with
arrows, loosed by a winged child floating high
above them.

Who flies with wings above in starry skies.

She leaned closer, mouth agape as the
words of the oracle came rushing back to her.
Every couple barbed with arrows was either in
an embrace or engaged in the act of passionate
lovemaking.

*And doth subdue each thing with fiery
flight.*

Revelation skirted the edges of her mind,
laboring her breath as she tried to make sense
of it. Could the prophecy have been a riddle, its
true meaning misinterpreted?

With a trembling hand, she reached for one
of the doors. She expected it to be impossible to
open, but it gave way easily, and she pushed it
open slowly.

She slipped inside, and with one soundless
step after another, she edged closer toward the
outline of a curtained bed. Even breathing from
her husband filled her ears. The mere sound of
it made her heart swell with a love so profound
she could hardly fathom it.

Eager to wake him, Psyche pulled the
curtain aside. When the lamp casted its soft

light upon the sleeping form inside, she nearly cried out.

Long, graceful limbs. Smooth, broad chest expanding and contracting. Soft, golden curls tousled over closed, long-lashed eyelids.

The scenes from the door collided with the image before her, and the truth was finally revealed. Her husband was no beast.

How could she have not put it together? Fiery flight meant one's journey into the heights of lust, into the heat of all-consuming passion. It was love that doth subdue, and each thing the heart of man.

She was not the wife of a winged serpent. She was the wife of Eros, the god of love.

Psyche stared in amazement, tears of joy welling in her eyes. He was larger than any mortal she had ever seen, and she supposed it only fitting for a god to be so. She surveyed the strong line of his jaw, admired the curving shape of his lips, and brought a hand to her mouth at the sight of the brilliant feathered wings that lay spread out behind him. He was the most beautiful thing she had ever seen, and she couldn't help herself when she leaned in to lovingly caress him.

Eros's eyes few open when the scalding oil from the lamp dripped onto his skin. His shocked gaze, as wide and blue as a cloudless sky, held hers.

"My love, you are as breathtaking as the light of dawn," whispered Psyche. "Why have you kept your beauty concealed for so long?"

She reached out again, to wipe away the oil that had seared his skin, but he caught her by the wrist.

"Because I wanted you to love me for the truth of my heart, not the beauty of my face," he said, pushing her away from him as he sat up.

Her brow furrowed at his harsh tone; at how tightly he gripped her wrist.

"But I do love you."

"And now that you have seen me? Has lust replaced that love?"

"It only makes my love stronger." Her gaze shifted to his hand, which was still wrapped painfully around her wrist. "I don't understand. Would you have me lie? Say I am not pleased the husband I thought to be a hideous beast is instead a god of immense power and beauty? I am only human."

"Yes, you are only human. And you have proven my mother right by disobeying me. I told you my rooms were forbidden to you."

88

"It is true I have disobeyed you, but I came to tell you I am sorry. That I love you no matter—"

"Silence! You have broken more than my trust, Psyche. You have broken my heart. Now I have no choice but to leave you for it; the pain is too great for me to bear." Eros drew himself up, his wings propelling him off the bed and out of her reach.

"No." She held her arm outstretched. "Please don't go. Stay with me, for I now see why you could not reveal the truth."

Eros turned to look at her, shaking his head sadly before saying, "I wish you had trusted me."

Brows drawn together with anger and agony at once, Eros's shoulders dropped. For a moment, Psyche thought he would stay, but when he touched the burn on his chest, sucking air in through his teeth from the pain, the stunning features he'd kept hidden from her hardened. When his jaw set and his eyes narrowed, she knew he would leave.

And after he climbed onto the sill and dove headlong into the sky without looking back, she knew she would never know true love again.

CHAPTER 12

EROS WATCHED HIS mother walk across one of Olympus's many gardens toward him. Prisms of light emanated from the crown of her golden hair like the finest cut crystal, her movements so fluid and graceful she seemed to float.

She came to a stop before him, but he did not look at her, too afraid she would see the torment in his eyes. It had been weeks since he'd flown to the top of the mountain in a rage. He preferred to be alone in his suffering, and so he'd avoided her in order to hide the wallowing that would follow. So that she would not see his anguish and insist on prying open healing wounds. But it seemed his attempt had been futile.

"My son. Why do you languish?"

There was no sense in hiding what he had done. He could keep nothing from her, always compelled to confess his misdeeds in time. Besides, with the inhabitants of Olympus's insatiable thirst for gossip and penchant for taking matters of indignation to Zeus, she would find out soon enough.

"I did not smite Psyche as you asked."

"I know," said his mother coolly.

Eros switched his gaze from the ground to his mother's face, and she answered his question before he could ask it.

"I am your mother. You were born unto this world as part of me. I bequeathed to you love and lust and passion so that you may be the guardian and keeper of hearts. Did you think I would not know when yours was broken?"

"Then why do you ask such a question?"

"Because I do not understand. You are a god. Why should your heart bleed for a human?"

His chest tightened. She spoke the truth, but he could not find the words to explain the bittersweet song that was love. The joy and torment, the elation and despair. "I should have listened."

"Yes." His mother nodded solemnly. "You should have. We are powerful, but we are not impervious."

He had been foolish, no doubt, and lamented his impulsive nature. Even so, he did not regret his time with what he knew in his heart to forever be his one and only true love. "Will you punish me?"

His mother's eyes softened. "No." An instant later, they hardened into the darkest aquamarine jewels. "But I will punish the girl."

Panic raced through Eros, the thought of Psyche enduring a terrible death almost making him shudder. Instead, he kept his emotions in check, so as not to stoke the embers of his mother's smoldering rage.

This conversation must end now. He stood, and though fear made his heart pound, he said, "Let her live out the rest of her days pining for the love she has lost. That will be punishment enough."

His mother contemplated his words as he held her gaze. Finally, she sighed. "I will do as you bid. Apart from this, you have served me well, my son, and have not caused me unrest. That is more than I can say for some of the others on this mountain."

Eros bowed his head, grateful. She'd agreed to leave Psyche to her misery, and although he was still angry at his mortal lover, he couldn't help but sigh with relief.

His mother laid a hand on his shoulder. "I will leave you to do your suffering in peace. But promise me you will consider seeking the company of another, a nymph perhaps."

She waited for a reply, but when her suggestion went ignored, her dazzling face hardened again. "You did not heed my previous warning and look at what happened to you. Indulge in whatever carnal pleasure you wish, so long as you forget Psyche exists. One more transgression and she *will* meet her end."

Eros did not seek the comfort found in a nymph's arms. Instead, he strolled through the gardens, gazed upon brilliant sunsets, and went about his task of shooting his arrows. All alone, and all without joy. Everything reminded him of her, and nothing would ever take her place.

The days continued to pass this way, as did the weeks, until Zeus called Eros to him. The god of love winged his way to the king's lavish throne room, and immediately upon entering, bent a knee. The king of the gods did not suffer fools gladly.

And I have been the biggest fool of all.

Eros lifted his head. "You called for me, my King?"

Zeus beckoned him forward. Eros obeyed without hesitation, his wings lifting him to his feet so that he could walk toward the king with haste. When he finally stood before the throne,

Eros peered up at the god of thunder. He was immense, with wide shoulders and thickly muscled arms. A ridged torso tapering and disappearing beneath the tunic wrapped around his waist, and even though his white hair was wild and unbound, his beard thick, he appeared regal.

"Eros," said Zeus, his voice deep and rumbling. "Aphrodite tells me you did not heed her warning. That you have consorted with a mortal woman."

"I have, but no longer. It was a mistake." Eros thought about going on to explain, but what more was there to say than that?

"Was it?" asked Zeus, tilting his head.

Eros took in the arch of one of Zeus's eyebrows, the purse of his lips, the slight curve of his... smile?

Zeus was no stranger to relationships with mortal women. He had been infatuated with scores of them, and there would no doubt be countless more to come. If anyone understood what Eros was going through, having to give up something so precious and dear, it was the ruler of Olympus.

"No." Eros shook his head. "I suppose the only mistake I've made is in thinking I could keep her with me."

"I have also made that mistake. My heart holds a place for all of the mortal treasures I could not keep. I have yet to learn my lesson." Zeus released a sigh. "Nonetheless, I have brought you here to seek council on a matter of great contention between Hera and I."

"How can I help you?"

"Have you any arrows that... lessen desire? Hera grows weary of my wandering eye. I fear she may be close to leading another coup. Perhaps you know a way to help me keep peace with my queen?"

Gold and lead. Love, lust, and passion or hate, revilement, and indifference. Those were the only two arrows with which Eros had to work his magic. Hera demanded that Zeus have eyes for her, and her alone. If Eros struck a leaden arrow into the heart of his king, all women would be rejected, including Hera. She would never have what she desired most, perhaps even more than fidelity; his love and devotion.

"I can impart only love or hate. I'm afraid the change of mind and heart you seek lies within your own hands, not mine."

Zeus nodded. "You speak the truth. I shall listen to your wise words and look within myself to see what might be changed.

Although, that might be an impossible task, one which I can make no promise to achieve. As for you, go now, god of love, and find another. A goddess, perhaps? Any one of them shall be proud to call such an honorable and handsome god husband."

Eros remained still as he accepted praise from Zeus. Yet, he wanted to run. He wanted to hide. Most of all, he wanted to lie. Just once. To tell himself that his heart would be whole again soon.

CHAPTER 13

PSYCHE WANDERED THROUGH the meadow. The sky, the gentle breeze, nor the sun's rays that kissed her cheeks could cheer her. Not even loving nudges from the velvet noses of forest animals could fill that hollow place in her heart.

Every day she wandered, through moss-covered trees, up grassy hills, and down into deep valleys. Anywhere that would take her far away from every night she spent in an empty palace weeping for Eros.

She had food and shelter, but she was utterly alone. Even her maids were gone, turned once more into butterflies.

On this evening, she sat beside a stream, its gurgling her only source of conversation. She was content to let it do the talking, for she had nothing left to say.

The sun hung low in the sky, brilliant shades of orange and pink just beginning to splash the horizon. She would head back soon, after the crickets serenaded her.

She turned when a twig snapped from behind her, expecting to see the white doe that came to console her often. She gasped when she saw a man walking toward her.

Heart pounding, Psyche quickly scrambled to her feet. She had not seen or spoken to anyone in weeks, perhaps even months, and she struggled to decide whether to run in fright or stay out of gratitude.

"I have seen you wander these lands for many days, always with such a long face," the man called out to her. "I've decided to cheer you with a song."

Even in the dim light, Psyche could see he wore a garland of greenery around his head, and her eyes widened when she spied curling horns just above his drooping ears. His face was bearded, and he looked to be middling in age, though bearing nary a trace of hardship or toil. His upper half was bare, broad-chested and finely muscled as any young man, perhaps even more so. But his bottom half was coated with thick, shaggy fur, and her gaze dropped to where his feet should have been.

Hooves.

Psyche turned to run. She'd heard the stories of how lustful satyrs were, and she was not about to fall prey.

"Wait! I only wish to soothe your soul." The satyr stopped his advance to hold up a flute.

"With my playing, not my lovemaking. I well know my nature, woman, but my intentions are pure."

The mirth in his voice calmed Psyche and, more curious now than frightened, she turned back toward the satyr, who had resumed his approach.

"How do you know my soul needs soothing?" she asked.

"It's in your eyes, in the dark circles that surround them. The sad pallor of your skin. Anyone with eyes can see it. Look at your reflection in the stream if you think me a liar."

Psyche's cheeks grew warm. It was true; she hadn't bathed in days, nor bothered to comb her hair. She could only imagine the sight. It must be alarming at best. "I don't think you a liar. I should be glad to hear you play."

The satyr nodded to a large rock before hopping onto it in a graceful leap. "Come, then, and I will soothe your soul."

Psyche took a seat in the grass before the satyr's stage, and he began to play. He blew a cheerful song, then another, his mouth moving masterfully over the instrument. Despite the heaviness of her being, her mood did lift, and she found herself smiling.

When the satyr finished, she clapped. He bowed and then hopped off the rock to join her in the grass.

"Now that your soul has been soothed, it is time to unburden your mind. A lover, is it? He has shattered your trust."

Psyche plucked a blade of grass, turning it in her fingers a few times before replying. "On the contrary. It is I who has broken trust. My true love has left me, and now I am nothing."

"Oh, that is not true. You are quite something as far as I can see. Dull with grief and despair at present, but a beauty of a gem underneath. What would it take to clear away the dirt and grime, so that you may shine?"

"I don't know that I can ever shine again."

"Who is this man that has taken the whole of your heart with him?"

"He is no man. He is Eros, the god of love."

"Ah, I see," said the satyr, chuckling heartily.

"Do you find the love between a god and a mortal so ridiculous?"

"Not in the least, my gem. Mortals are hard to resist."

"Who are you?"

"I am Pan. God of mountain wilds."

"Soother of souls," said Psyche, quirking her lips into a grin.

"Indeed. In more ways than one." Pan winked. "Have you called out to the god of love? Perhaps his heart can be plied with prayer and repentance.

"Many times. It is no use. He refuses to listen."

"Hmm." Pan stroked his beard. "Have you tried appealing to his mother, the goddess of love, then?"

Shaking her head, Psyche replied, "No, she will not hear me. In fact, she would just as soon strike me dead. I have affronted the great goddess. Not intentionally, but she will not help me, nonetheless. A mother is always incensed on her son's behalf, and I have broken his heart."

"Your regret is plain. So why not put your fear aside and ask the goddess for guidance? Surely, she knows where her son has gone. If she would smite you, then so be it. Would living the rest of your days in sorrow be more bearable than dying for love? I know the thoughts you have entertained; fill your lungs with water from the very river that flows not far from here. Where is the sense in that? Hope springs eternal. Hermes saw to that."

The mountain god had a point. The great messenger of the gods had felt pity for the mortals when Zeus had created Pandora's box. Where others had given devastation and ruin to be unleashed, Hermes' gift to humanity had been hope.

An idea began to take shape in Psyche's head. "Can you take me to Aphrodite?"

Pan tilted his head, placing a hand over his heart. "Sadly, I am not an Olympian, and not allowed to tread upon the rocks of Mount Olympus unless summoned." He offered her his palm. "But you have only to take my hand and I will bring you to the steps of Aphrodite's temple in Corinth."

Psyche gnawed at the inside of her lip, contemplating the god's offer. Should she risk Aphrodite's wrath, which would undoubtedly be two-fold given what havoc Psyche had wreaked?

The image of a sleeping Eros made her heart beat faster, and the memory of his touch made her stomach flutter. Yes, love was infinitely sweeter than sorrow, and what she would not do to tell Eros how sorry she was, that he possessed all of her heart, even still. What she would not give to hear his voice one more time?

Her life, she decided. She would ask Aphrodite to help her win back the love of Eros. If the cost was her last breath, then so be it.

Psyche took hold of Pan's outstretched hand. Her belly dipped and swirled as he smiled at her, and it was the last thing she saw before the world around her disappeared.

CHAPTER 14

IN THE BLINK of an eye, Psyche stood before the temple of Aphrodite. There was a burnished glow over everything, and the soft coo of mourning doves came from somewhere atop the magnificent stone structure. The rising sun and the golden stillness of it all was truly breathtaking, but that was not the reason she could scarcely draw in air.

When she noticed a basket of roses in her hand, Psyche blew out a breath. The satyr had seen to it she had an offering for the goddess, and she inhaled gratefully.

Psyche steadied herself and entered the temple. A great statue of Aphrodite looked down on her, and now a looping and swirling stomach ailed her, not a heaving chest.

As she approached, she spied dried roses and small honey jars laying at the base of the pedestal, along with sweet cakes and rotting fruit. The offerings had attracted worshipers of both the crawling and winged sort.

She brushed the brittle petals and crumbling cakes aside, then carefully arranged the freshly cut flowers, reserving several to lay across the feet of the statue.

Once finished, she went down on her knees and began to pray.

"I beg you to forgive me, goddess, for I did not willfully seek to contest your beauty."

The silence was deafening, and the sting of tears accompanied a swelling in her throat. To be forgiven for the past was not why she had come.

"I know the sorrow that consumes my head may be trivial, but the love that fills my heart is great," she continued, clasping her hands tighter. "Hear me, goddess, and come to me. It is no secret to me that gods can walk upon the Earth in the flesh. I beg you to grace me with your presence, so that I may hear from your sacred lips where my love has gone, and if there is anything to be done to appease him."

Psyche closed her eyes, listening for the slightest sound that Aphrodite had heard her. But there was no murmur of rustling cloth, no whisper of sighing breath. There was nothing, and despair overtook her.

"*Please.* I will do anything," she begged, squeezing her lids shut so her tears would not escape. This was no time to show mortal weakness.

She waited, but when she was met with more silence, she opened her eyes and looked upon the face of the statue. "I will do anything."

The resulting silence was too much to bear, and Psyche lowered her head, her hope dropping with it. When her gaze landed on the offerings, she reached out with trembling fingers.

As if she were floating high above, she watched her hand pick up the jar and throw it, so that it shattered against the stone. Trance broken, she snatched up the largest piece and held it to her wrist. "Including death. If you will not help me then I will sacrifice my life. *I would rather die than live without him.*"

Psyche gasped from the pain of the jagged edge of broken clay biting into her skin, but before she could drag it across her wrist, a rose landed on the ground in front of her.

She looked up, the shard dropping from her hand when she met the eyes of the goddess standing in the flesh before her, glaring down at her from atop her stone dais.

Psyche's hair rose, and her skin prickled as she cowered beneath the goddess, who continued to stare at her in silence. She remained frozen in place, unsure of what to do next. Her heart pounded in her ears when

Aphrodite raised her arm and the temple grew dark. Psyche slowly turned to face the direction in which the goddess was pointing.

A mound of grain sprung up from the ground like a geyser, growing in size until it blocked the entrance of the temple almost completely.

When only a few rays of golden light where able to make their way in, Aphrodite finally spoke. "If I am to help you sort out your matter with my son, you must show the same courtesy. Separate this grain as you would your impatience from your patience, for love deserves only the latter. You have until the next sunrise to finish, or I will consider you unworthy and speak to you no more."

When Psyche turned to face Aphrodite, the goddess was once again a statue.

Psyche bit back a sob at the impossible task before her—a test she was meant to fail. But she had claimed she would do anything, and if this would prove her worthy of Aphrodite's help—of Eros's love—Psyche would do it.

She knelt in front of the pile of grain and began to work.

Sweat dampened Psyche's brow. After sitting back on her heels, she wiped her forehead with the back of a hand. Her shoulders ached, her fingers were sore, and her vision had begun to blur, from strain or sweat or tears, she couldn't be sure. The only thing she was certain of was that human hands could not achieve this task, even with a strong will to urge them on.

She had been picking at the grains all day, separating them into three smaller piles of rice, bulgur, and millet as fast as she could, but it hadn't been enough. The sun was setting, and the mound looked as though she hadn't touched it at all.

Tears sprang to her eyes, and her sob echoed through the temple as she hung her head and wept. The image of her sleeping husband came into her mind, bringing with it the memory of his gentle voice and loving touch, and it made her tears fall harder.

Until she felt the tickle of tiny legs marching across her hand.

Psyche examined the ant crawling up the length of her finger, wiping away the tears as she watched the insect traverse down the other side and into her palm. Despite her feelings of hopelessness, she smiled as she lowered her hand to the ground.

"I am far too big to be a crumb. Go about your work, little one, so that I may continue mine."

The ant walked off her fingertip and headed toward the grain. Psyche sighed, gathering the strength to move her sore limbs once again when something caught her eye.

The pile was writhing.

A black mass swarmed over every inch of the grain, and she watched in wonder as countless ants picked up a single grain before falling in line to carry it to one of the three smaller piles she'd made. Each pile had grown bigger in the short time she had stopped to despair.

Understanding immediately, Psyche unleashed an elated cry. "The battle is not lost!" She crawled on hands and knees over to the grain. "How foolish I have been to waste precious time lamenting. You have been sent to me, my little soldiers, by whom I do not know, but I am glad you are here."

With the aid of a battalion of insects, Psyche worked tirelessly throughout the night. Her hope restored and her determination renewed, the mound of grain shrank until, finally, just before dawn, the task was complete.

"Thank you, my friends. I will be forever grateful," whispered Psyche, sagging against one of the temple's pillars to wait for the goddess of love to arrive.

No sooner had she uttered the words when an imposing figure, backlit by the sun and casting a shadow on the stone floor before her, stepped into the temple.

Psyche stood straighter, ready to discuss the whereabouts of her lost love. But the shocked look on the goddess's face when she saw the grain had been separated caused Psyche to take a step backward. The angry expression the goddess sent her way made Psyche want to run.

"How?" demanded Aphrodite, clearly displeased. "That task was impossible for human hands to achieve. Reveal to me who has helped you."

Despite being in the presence of a divinity, with power to wield over humanity when and however she pleased, Psyche seethed at the goddess's admission. Fear drained away, replaced by the courage only anger could evoke, and she took a brave step forward. "Have you misjudged my will, oh great goddess of beauty?"

"Answer my question, mortal. Which of us have you called upon for help?" Aphrodite's gaze searched the ceiling of her temple, as though she would find the culprit there.

"I do not deny that I had help," replied Psyche, "but I did not ask for it. It came to me freely and I accepted, for there was no mention I could not do so should I receive a helping hand. Only the assumption that no one would offer."

Aphrodite's gaze dropped to Psyche's sandaled feet, prompting her to look down as well. She discovered several ants crawling across the tops of her feet.

The golden-haired goddess's eyes flitted to where the daunting pile of grain had been, then down at the ants before returning to Psyche's face.

"Demeter," murmured Aphrodite, and for a moment, the wide flare of her nostrils was in stark contrast with the thin line of her pursed lips. Knowing she had been bested, the hard angle of one brow transformed into a graceful arch. "It seems the goddess of the grain harvest has taken enough pity on you to help you complete the task which I have set before you."

Psyche remained quiet, even though she wanted to scream.

With a wave of Aphrodite's hand, the piles of grain Psyche had spent day and night separating disappeared. Her heart sank at how easily the goddess could dismiss every bit of her hard work in an instant. Aphrodite truly was as cruel as she was beautiful, and the fear she would decide to dismiss Psyche's life just as easily made her quake.

"I have no control over who takes pity on mortals." Aphrodite moved closer, beginning to walk a circle around Psyche and the pillar she held onto for support. "It is no matter. I shall give you another task to prove your worth."

The power emanating from the goddess pricked Psyche's skin like so many wasps, and she pushed away from the pillar in an attempt to alleviate the stinging.

"Love is not for the weak. It takes strength to give it unconditionally." Aphrodite continued along her path around the pillar, her gaze fixed ahead of her rather than on Psyche. "Some would even argue bravery is required. Let us see how strong you are, how brave."

Psyche took a stumbling step backward, watching how the air around the goddess shimmered and waved as she approached the very place where Psyche had been standing only moments ago.

"Bring me a hank of fleece from Chrysomallus, the golden ram of Colchis," said Aphrodite before passing behind the pillar.

Psyche opened her mouth to ask how long she had, but when the goddess did not appear on the other side, she closed it.

CHAPTER 15

PSYCHE HURRIED OUT of the temple and begin to walk. Chrysomallus could be found in Colchis, but how long would it take to reach him traveling on foot, she didn't know. Regardless, there was no time to be wasted. She would ask a passerby if she encountered one. Perhaps they would also be kind enough to escort her there.

The midday sun beat down, pinking her skin and parching her tongue. She had no idea if she was walking in the right direction, but that problem could wait. She would be headed in no direction if she did not find water first.

Psyche followed the sound of a rushing stream, keeping her eye out for wild berries to eat along the way. She had indeed happened upon a patch when she heard a flute in the distance. Shoving a handful of the juicy morsels into her mouth, she headed toward the music, intent on finding its source.

A man sat on a rock by the bank of the bubbling stream. The strap of his satchel cut across his back, and the song he played sounded familiar. When Psyche saw his drooping goat ears, she broke out into a run.

"Pan!" she shouted. "God of the mountain wilds, soother of souls, it is I, Psyche!"

Pan stopped playing and stood. A wide smile broke out across his bearded face when their eyes met, and the warmth of it made her run faster.

"We meet again, my gem," said Pan, laughing heartily.

The sound soothed Psyche's soul to hear it, and when she reached the satyr, she threw her arms around him. "I am glad to see you."

Pan imparted a quick pat on her back before breaking her embrace to clutch her by the shoulders. "I see the goddess of beauty has decided against a swift and terrible death. I do say, I am quite relieved, but I must know... Did she grant you your request? Are you privy to the whereabouts of your god of love? Tell me all, my precious gem."

"She let me live," replied Psyche, stepping out of the satyr's grasp and toward the stream to slake her thirst. "But she did not tell me where to find Eros. Not yet."

Pan rushed after her, half running, half skipping. "Whatever does that mean?" He stood over her, stamping a hooved foot impatiently as she dipped her hand into the water and brought the clear, cool liquid to her lips. "Details! Details! Oh, the gods can be sly if not tricky. Who should know that better than I?"

"Aphrodite bid me to separate a pile of grain as tall as the temple before she would consider discussing the matter with me," explained Psyche as she made her way over to the rock and sat down. Her brow angled at the strange feeling that suddenly washed over her. The satyr. The stream. The rock. Hadn't she been here before?

"Impossible work!" Pan hopped up to sit beside her. "She thought you would fail, but clearly you did not. How did you do it?"

"With the help of some friends. Ants sent by Demeter, to help me separate the grain." Psyche beamed, feeling lighter than she had in a long time. "Speaking of help from friends..."

"Of course, I will help you, in any way, but what can a lowly god of field and stream do?

"Send me to Colchis. I must procure a hank of golden fleece."

Pan's eyes widened. "From Chrysomallus?"

Psyche nodded, to which Pan shook his head.

"Oh, my gem. He is the wildest and most dangerous of all."

"I do not ask for help with the task outright. No, Aphrodite would not be pleased with that. I must procure the fleece myself. The journey, however, would take too long on foot, or even by chariot."

"I shall send you there, yes, but how will you retrieve the golden fleece without assistance? Chrysomallus is of a nasty sort. He would surely not hand over his fleece willingly."

"I supposed that is my riddle to solve."

"Hmm." Pan quirked his lips as he scrubbed his chin, pondering. "How to calm the horribly wretched ram so the precious gem can steal a hank of his golden fleece? A riddle indeed."

"What if I simply ask him for it?" Psyche's brow crumpled, wondering now, too, how best to complete her next impossible task.

"He is wild and dangerous." Pan took off the small leather satchel he wore and handed it over to Psyche. "He spends his days butting heads with his brethren on an island that stands in the middle of a river. I doubt he would stop and listen to the likes of a mortal."

Psyche bit the inside of her lip, the light feeling she'd had earlier growing heavy again. She accepted the satchel with a furrowed brow.

"You'll need something to carry the golden fleece to Aphrodite."

"You are right," said Psyche, adjusting the strap until it rested comfortably between her shoulder blades. "But how do you suppose—"

Before she could finish, a dazed look overtook Pan's face, as though he were in a trance, and he murmured the words, "Slumber comes when the wind blows... making your wish come true in dreams."

Pan shook himself, clearing his throat. "Sorry about that. What were we talking about?"

Psyche folded her arms, irritated at the interruption. "How to get my hands on some golden fleece without perishing. Your babbling like a brook is not helpful. I seek answers, not more riddles."

"If we are to remain the friends we are, you should know that I am often compelled to speak in riddles and rhymes. I cannot help it. They come to me unannounced, and I must simply blurt them out."

Psyche softened. She liked Pan, and he had agreed to take her to Colchis. "Do you at least know what they mean?"

Pan shrugged "Alas, I have never been good at knowing what they mean... or at solving them."

Psyche sighed at his toothy grin. Then she took the hand he held out to her, and, just as it did before, the world fell away.

CHAPTER 16

PSYCHE SHIELDED HER eyes from the sun glinting off the narrow river before her. Its current flowed slow and lazy, and the weeping willows on its banks dipped their long, diaphanous branches into its muddy waters.

The loud crack of clashing horns drew her eyes to an island a short distance downriver. She winced with every impact and cringed at each eerie wail that followed.

She quietly made her way toward the horrible sounds until she came to a spot lined with reeds, thick enough for her to crouch low and watch without being seen.

Chrysomallus was not only brilliantly hued but winged, and he stood proud, wings spread out like a bird of prey as he waited for his next opponent to challenge him. Sired by Poseidon and born from the nymph Theophone, he was a beautiful thing, there was no doubt about that.

Not willing to admit her idea of reasoning with the creature might not be the most prudent, she stood, ready to call out to him and explain her plight, when an enraged bellow ripped through the air. Psyche pushed the reeds aside for a better look. What she saw next made her wish she hadn't; Chrysomallus was mauling one of his own with his golden hooves.

It was a bloody scene, and Psyche let go of the stalks to cover her eyes, so that she would not have to witness another moment of it. But she could still hear the pained and tortured cries, even over the pounding in her ears. Pan had been right; approaching the beast was out of the question.

Psyche crawled further back on the soggy bank to think. How could she subdue Chrysomallus long enough to snatch a handful of his golden fleece? A gentle breeze blew, bending the reeds ever so slightly as she mulled the thought over in her mind.

Could she create a diversion of some sort? Should she risk angering Aphrodite by asking for help from another?

The wind began to blow.

Perhaps she could wait until nightfall. But what if the golden ram never slept? What would she do then?

The wind began to blow harder, this time with enough force to set the reeds whistling. It was a beautiful, soothing sound, and it reminded her of Pan's flute. Thinking of him brought to mind the words of the strange riddle he'd been compelled to speak aloud.

Slumber comes when the wind blows...

Psyche closed her eyes and listened to the wind play music on the reeds. She began to sway, letting the peaceful moment calm her mind. No clashing skulls. No terrible bellows. No cries of pain...

Her eyes flew open, and she clambered over to the reeds to push them aside.

Chrysomallus had stopped battling and was now staggering about. The others, who had already settled down into the grass, rested their heads on their woolly breasts.

The wind picked up and the reeds grew louder. The golden ram dropped to the ground with a grunt, his head bobbing and nodding until, finally, he collapsed on his side with a great snort.

Making your wish come true in dreams.

Psyche's mouth dropped open as she realized the answer to Pan's riddle.

"Glory and praise to you, benevolent Zephyrus," she whispered, waiting until the beast's snoring came at even intervals before wading through the reeds and out into the open.

This was it, the answer. So long as the wind god kept blowing on the reeds, she could safely retrieve a hank of golden fleece from Chrysomallus while he dreamed. But she must not dawdle. No, she must act quickly so as to not squander this gift from Zephyrus.

The water was up to her waist now, the muck squishing between her toes with every step. She halted, nearly crying out when something under the surface slithered across the back of her leg. She inhaled a breath, steadying herself, then checked to make sure the leather satchel still floated behind her before resuming her watery trek toward the island.

She moved as quietly through the murky water as its lapping and rippling would allow. When she reached the bank of the island where Chrysomallus lay sleeping, she slowly climbed the rocks lying just below its grassy shore.

The golden ram was even larger now that she saw him up close. So massive was he, her legs refused to move, insisting on shaking instead. She lay a hand on the satchel, to open its flap in preparation, when something flashed in the bushes that grew just beyond where Chrysomallus lay snoring.

A clump of golden fleece hung on a branch, floating in the breeze and sparkling in the sunlight.

Psyche bit down on her lip to stop her sheer delight from waking the ram. Aphrodite hadn't said how much of the fleece Psyche would need to bring to her, only that she must bring her some.

Legs still trembling but resigned to move forward and be done with the task, Psyche crept around Chrysomallus and toward the bush on which her salvation hung. When she reached her golden prize, she plucked it from the branch ever so carefully and tucked it inside the satchel. Then, with her lungs hardly working, she began her slow journey back to the bank.

She winced when she stepped down into the muck, wishing she was already at the other side of the river. Though she held her arms out for balance, it was no use against the slime that grew on the rocks below, and she cried out when her foot slipped, causing her to go tumbling into the water.

The splash woke Chrysomallus, and he was on his feet in an instant, heavy golden hooves pounding the ground like thunder as he ran toward her with murderous intent. Psyche did not stifle her scream of terror, and it ripped out of her until her throat burned from the force of it.

She dove into the river, arms flailing and legs kicking as fast as they would go. She heard Chrysomallus bellow at the edge of the island, enraged. When she turned to see if he would follow her into the river, she saw him first rear in outrage, then take out his impotent wrath on the earth by pawing and tearing out great chunks of sod.

He must be forbidden to leave the island. Relieved, Psyche coughed and sputtered from the dirty water that had infiltrated her lungs during her wild clamber for safety. She collapsed on the other side of the river and had barely the time to catch her breath when a shadow blocked out the sun.

Psyche looked up to see Aphrodite standing over her, face hard, eyes piercing. Psyche shifted to her knees, willing herself to stop the nearly uncontrollable shaking of her limbs. It would not serve her well for the goddess to think she was afraid, when in fact, she was only shivering because she was dripping wet and cold.

Twice now she had proven her worth, and she was growing less afraid and more certain the goddess would have no other choice but to help her.

Psyche slid a hand into the satchel and pulled out the gleaming hank of fleece. Without a word, she stood and held it out to Aphrodite. The goddess lashed out at her audacity by smacking the fleece out of her hand.

"You wretched thing. Why do you persist?"

"Because I love him. And I know he loves me. Because heart and soul should not be apart."

"You enrage me so. Yet I cannot help myself from being impressed by your tenacity. I have tested your patience and your courage. Let us see about your cunning."

No sooner did Aphrodite finish the words when the sound of a powerful rush of water filled Psyche's ears. She spun around to see a wonderous sight; a towering waterfall, with black water flowing from a dark cave and cascading down the side of a great, gray mountain.

"Bring me water from the place where the Styx falls away from the realm of the gods and into the world of mortals. Do this and your trials may soon be over."

CHAPTER 17

ONCE AGAIN, THE goddess vanished, leaving Psyche alone in turmoil. Would these tests ever end? Was this some kind of torturous game that Aphrodite would play until old age sapped Psyche's strength and wits? Just thinking about it made her jaw clench almost as tightly as her fists, and she nearly gave in to the urge to tear out her hair.

"I am worthy!" shouted Psyche, unable to stop the words from bursting forth. She lifted her gaze to the sky and whispered. "You will see."

Still panting, she peered up at the mountain, assessing the difficulty of her next task. There was no path that led up to the waterfall. She would have to scale sheer rock walls; jamming her fingers into shallow cracks and gripping outcroppings with her toes. Provided she did not slip and fall to her death, what vessel did she have with which to carry her charge to Aphrodite?

Psyche closed her eyes and rubbed her throbbing temples. It seemed as though, of all the tasks she had been given, this might be the most impossible.

The sound of her husband's laughter echoed through her aching head just then. The rich register of it rang in her ears, and it brought with it a fresh wave of resolve. She would do anything to hear him laugh again, to feel her cheeks flush from bringing her love such delight with her playful quips.

Psyche sprinted to the base of the mountain and began to climb. She grunted like a wild boar each time she pulled herself up, panting like worn out prey when she stopped to gather strength for the next round of her ascent.

The higher she climbed, the fiercer and colder the wind became, punishing her with her own long strands of hair by whipping them into her face. Her fingers went numb, her toes already bleeding from scraping against the sharp edges of rock.

Many hours later, Psyche sighed with exhaustion as she crawled onto a small plateau to rest. She looked down over the edge, then quickly flung herself backward, clinging to the mountain so she wouldn't accidentally go tumbling over. It felt like she had been climbing for days. In reality, she discovered, she had ascended no more than a few hundred feet. A fall from this height would surely kill her, but there was still so much farther to go.

She craned her neck upward to survey the distance. The mist from the waterfall continued to dampen her clothes, which were now nothing more than filthy and torn rags, without sympathy. Psyche dropped her head, contemplating whether or not to curl in on herself for warmth. Several drops left small, dark circles on the rocks near her feet. Whether they were from her dripping hair or weeping eyes, she couldn't find the energy to care.

"Eros, oh, my heart," said Psyche, praying aloud even though the wind stole the sound. "I fear we shall never meet again, for this may be a test I cannot pass. So, I must tell you now that which I cannot say to your divine being in person. I am sorry, with all my heart, and I beg for your forgiveness. If you cannot forgive me, then I hope one day you will at least remember the tenderness of our love, the trueness. I will forever and always—"

An eagle's cry pierced the wind.

Psyche clung to the rocky wall as she watched the enormous bird circle in the sky above her. She twisted her body, hugging the stone closer when the eagle dove at her, a gust of wind tousling her hair as it flew past her with great speed. With that flinching movement, something within her satchel pressed into her ribs. Confused, she pulled the bag from her side to examine its sudden and mysterious contents.

A jar, with a stopper to keep whatever it held from spilling out, and two coins the likes of which she had never seen.

The eagle cried again, louder this time, before doubling back and heading straight for her. Psyche shrank in terror when it landed a scant few feet from her, keeping its wings spread for balance in the treacherous wind.

This was no ordinary eagle, that was plain. It was larger, much larger, and shone like the finest of precious metals, as if it had been dipped in molten gold.

The eagle of Zeus.

Holding out a razor-sharp talon, the golden bird screamed again. Terrified and trembling, Psyche crouched before the enormous creature. Had Zeus heard her instead of Eros, growing weary of her futile attempts at a reunion and sending this divine symbol of his power to put her out of her misery?

The eagle unleashed another cry, then suddenly took flight. It soared over to the waterfall, dove low, and flew along the edge, dragging a talon along the black water to send up a foaming white spray.

Understanding caused Psyche to jump to her feet, despite the danger the quick and sudden motion presented. She wrenched open the satchel, pulled out the water jar, and removed the stopper before carefully setting it at the edge of the plateau. Gratitude filled her heart once more, welling then bubbling out of her in the form of laughter when the golden eagle swooped down to snatch it.

Psyche watched as it clutched the jar in one great talon and flew to the waterfall. It dipped the jar into the black water, and Psyche reached out her hands to catch the jar when the eagle flew low and dropped it. The jar landed in her waiting hands, only a little of the water sloshing out, and she immediately secured it with the cork.

The eagle's massive wings lifted it higher into the sky, and Psyche looked on in awe as it passed through the clouds and disappeared into the heavens that lay beyond. Glad for her luck, Psyche placed the jar inside the satchel and went to make her way back down the mountain when there came a voice.

"It seems as though you have not only drawn the attention of mortals but have curried the favor of gods. Patience, strength, cunning... You have passed every test I have set before you. But not without pity from the highest among us, Zeus himself, a matter of fact I cannot control. And, so, I must acquiesce."

Psyche drew in a sharp breath. Finally, she would know how to reach Eros, her friend, her lover... her husband.

"I will speak to my son on your behalf, vouching for your sincerity and urging him to return to you." The goddess appeared, floating larger than life in the air before Psyche, with shining waves of hair rippling languidly despite the harsh mountain winds.

"But first, you must do one last thing for me. These tests have left me feeling rather drained and dull. I must be refreshed, and who better to help the goddess of beauty than one who has proven herself so worthy? Replace the water in your jar with a beauty elixir made from the dew of spring flowers, a remedy for my ailment only the Queen of the Underworld can provide."

"The Underworld?" asked Psyche, incredulous. "No mortal has ever ventured into the realm of Hades and come back to the land of the living to tell the tale."

Aphrodite tilted her head. "But you have been so resourceful. Surely you can achieve it. Think of how heartened Eros will be to know that you have done such a great favor for his mother."

"I know of no entrance into the spirit world other than death. How will I find it?"

The fabric of the goddess's golden threads, held in place by a dazzling golden girdle, swirled as she moved.

"Why, it is there," she said, pointing to the dark cave from which the waterfall flowed. "I will even spirit you there myself if you agree, so that you may not waste time climbing the rest of the way."

Psyche swallowed hard, already knowing her answer. She would go into the Underworld for whatever Aphrodite wanted, no matter the cost, and the knowledge of that certainty dropped into the pit of her stomach. Would she be able to convince Persephone, bride of Hades, goddess of spring, queen of all who—and what—dwelled below ground, to hold audience with her, a mere mortal?

In spite of her doubt, Psyche squared her shoulders, steeling herself for what lay ahead. She must try. If not for the sake of reuniting with Eros then to see her fate, whatever it may be, through to the end.

"I will honor your last request and bring you the elixir of spring, goddess. But when I return from the realm of the dead, you must promise to honor mine."

Aphrodite's lips curled into the faintest hint of a smile, but her aquamarine eyes flashed brightly. "You have my word."

Psyche gasped in disbelief at the binding words that came out of the goddess's mouth. If Psyche retrieved the elixir, Aphrodite would send Eros to her. Psyche had been careful with her demand, allowing no room for double meaning or trickery. Aphrodite would have to honor her vow.

Both pride at having achieved such a cunning deal and uncertainty that perhaps it hadn't been wise to negotiate with a goddess raced through Psyche with equal force, making her legs shaky and weak. The resigned look on Aphrodite's face should have been a good sign that the bargain between mortal and goddess had been well struck.

Why, then, did Psyche feel like it was the worst of omens?

CHAPTER 18

PSYCHE PEERED INTO the cave. The stone was glossy obsidian, the sand was as dusky as the night sky, and the water that flowed from within was the black of emptiness.

The wind whistled, an eerie sound that was almost as desolate as Aphrodite's voice. "Go now, mortal, and fetch for me the elixir. You will be rewarded once I hold it in my hands."

Psyche shivered, the hair at the back of her neck rising at the taunt lying just below the surface of the goddess's words. What seemed like plain enough speech by the gods was usually a riddle; a twist on meaning that worked solely to their advantage.

Psyche pushed the thought from her mind. She had outwitted the goddess, left no room for trickery. All Psyche needed to do was bring the goddess her elixir, then the trials would be over.

But with Psyche's first step toward the cave, Aphrodite imparted something else. "Do not open the jar once you have it. Bring it straight to me."

Psyche struggled to bite her tongue. So many demands. Hadn't the goddess already asked for enough? Determined not to show her irritation, Psyche nodded, indicating she understood, and started toward the yawning mouth of the cave.

The banks on either side of the river were narrow but widened the farther she walked into the darkness. This place was a void, a sad nothingness, draining the hope from her and replacing it with despair.

The gray mist floating up from the black water shed just enough ambient light so that Psyche did not trip over the uneven ground as she moved farther into the Underworld. The temperature began to rise, the muggy air causing her hair and clothes to stick to her clammy skin.

Psyche nearly lost her balance when a strange fog arose from the ground a short distance in front of her. It seemed to have a life of its own as it billowed and rolled, and she stifled a scream she knew would do her no good. It continued its advance until it swirled and eddied a mere arm's length before her. When the fog settled and fell to the ground once more, it revealed a cloaked figure, face hooded in shadow, holding an oar in its bony hand.

Without a word, the figure turned away from her and began to walk along the rocky shore. Psyche followed, clutching onto the strap of her satchel as if it would lend any kind of protection should she need it.

They walked for what seemed like days. Although she couldn't see much, Psyche could feel the river had widened into a vast and rippling lake, the sound of its waves echoing off the cavern walls. She did not ask questions, for she knew who the figure was and where he was leading her. The ferryman, Charon, had come to take her across the Styx.

They continued in silence until, finally, they came to a dock. The small wooden boat, dark with rot and hardly fit to carry an infant without falling apart, bobbed at the end of its tether.

Charon turned to face her once more. He tamped the handle of the long oar, which looked to be made of the same mossy and rotted wood as the boat, into the pebbles before holding out his hand to collect payment.

Of course, Psyche had been wondering what she would offer him the entire time they had been walking. She could think of nothing but her life or her soul, but she would need those once she found Eros. Would the ferryman accept the satchel? Perhaps he could use it to hold the coins...

The answer bloomed into being like a summer rose in the sun. The odd coins she'd discovered on the mountainside. She opened her satchel and felt around for them.

"Gods above, please let them still be here."

Her fingers connected with the two round coins and she pulled them out with a smile. Taking a step closer to the ghoulish Charon, whose gaunt face she could now see clearly. He stared back at her with vacant eyes. Oh, what a horror it must be, to be fated to do such work.

"There you are, fine sir," she beamed, determined to bring a bit of cheer to both their circumstances. "Payment for the crossing. And I don't mind rowing if you wish it so. It must be awfully tiresome to—"

The hollow of Charon's eyes flared a searing red. She heard the oar creak under the pressure of the ferryman's grip, and for a moment she thought he might reach out and choke her, maybe even slap her. But when one side of his lipless mouth slid up into a half-grin, she relaxed.

But not much, for now he was pointing at the rickety vessel tied to the end of the dock. She swallowed hard before stepping onto the gray, worm-eaten planks. What other means did she have to make her way to Persephone, queen of the dark?

She stepped into the boat and sat, gripping the rough edge of the sagging seat for balance while Charon unlashed the rope and pushed away from the dock and into the dark and foreboding waters of the Styx.

Steam stinking of sulfur rose from the churning waters, the smell of it burning the inside of Psyche's nose. From this, she surmised the water was not only rough, but deadly, and tried to remain calm when an image of herself flailing in agony while her skin melted off her bones formed in her mind. She was unsuccessful at stifling a terrified cry, however, when an enormous tentacle broke the surface and wiggled its way up the side of the small boat, snaking straight for her.

Charon's oar came down hard on the slimy appendage of the menacing beast writhing below the ominous waters, and it was gone.

Psyche pressed a hand to her chest. "I am most grateful for that!"

Charon nodded at her solemnly and continued to row.

Crossing the Styx seemed to be devoid of time or space. It felt much like how Psyche imagined floating in the womb might feel. She was surrounded by darkness, the air was heavy and humid, and sound, save for water splashing against Charon's oar, was muffled by the mist.

Psyche found a strange calmness in the absence of those things. It gave her time to think, to analyze... to strategize. Was this truly her last test? What would she do if it wasn't? What direction should she go once she got to the other side?

The answer to every question was simple: Keep moving forward, for she could not turn back.

The fog suddenly grew thicker, engulfing her so that she could not see her own hand in front of her face. She whimpered as the sense of something massive and unknown approached. Gooseflesh puckered the skin of her arms, raising the hair there and causing her to shiver, even in the oppressive heat.

The boat lurched forward, halted by an unseen shore, and Psyche stood once the bow was steady. Charon appeared on the shore next to the boat, holding his oar in one hand and stretching the other out to her. She reached for the ferryman's hand. It was cool and dry, and surprisingly gentle.

Pebbles crunched beneath her bare feet—for she had lost her sandals some time back—as she made her way up shore. She turned to ask Charon where she could find the king and queen of the Underworld, but there was no trace of the ferryman or his vessel. Psyche pulled in a deep breath, supposing she shouldn't have expected anything more from him.

She continued farther inland, if one could call the belly of the Underworld that. She had hardly traversed it, so perhaps she was only in the throat, on the verge of being swallowed whole. Psyche came up to what looked to be three more dark mouths.

Entrances that most likely led to the bowels.

She felt a pull towards the center passage and entered. She said a silent prayer that it would lead her straight to the heart of the Underworld. To Hades and Persephone.

Psyche felt her way down the tunnel. Water dripped in the distance, and she tripped several times, dashing her palms and knees against the sharp rocks. She could not see the gashes her falls left, only feel the warm trickle of blood that flowed from them.

There were all sorts of smaller passageways that branched off the main tunnel, but Psyche stayed the course, slowly making her way forward. She had stopped to bandage a cut on her knee that refused to stop bleeding and had just ripped off a strip of her tattered dress to do so, when torchlight flickered on the walls of one of the tunnels that riddled the main path.

Then came a sniff. Then another, deeper, followed by a low moan.

Psyche jumped up, abandoning her work to crouch behind the large rock she had been sitting on. Safely hidden within the shadows, she peeked over the top of her hiding spot, which she just barely had time to procure. Terror gripped her, squeezing her chest as she watched an enormous creature, possessing only one eye but owning a mouthful of pointed teeth, lumber into view.

The cyclops stood before her, head moving from side to side as it sniffed the air. Its giant eye was open, reflecting the flames of the torch as it searched frantically for the source of the scent it was tracking. It howled with rage when it was unable to locate it.

Psyche knew she must act, and quickly if she was going to escape the bone-crushing grip of this ravenous beast of Gaia and Uranus.

And then she saw it, a small crack in the rock behind the cyclops, big enough for a mortal to fit through yet small enough to keep the towering creature out.

But how would she get to it?

Thinking fast, she pressed the piece of cloth she'd ripped from her dress to her bleeding knee. Still holding his torch, the cyclops grunted, locking in on the scent of her blood and ambling towards her. Quick as lightning, Psyche tossed the blood-soaked rag a few feet in front of where she crouched. When the one-eyed monster's attention was diverted, she dove in the opposite direction, into the shadows the torchlight could not reach and dashed toward the crack in the cavern wall.

Psyche crawled on her hands and knees through the tiny passageway without looking back, believing the angry bellows and frustrated clashes of rock upon rock when they told her the cyclops hadn't been able to pursue her. A torrent of tears threatened to burst from her eyes, but she held them in check.

Eros, my love, I am coming... Nothing can stop me, for I will not turn back now... or ever.

CHAPTER 19

THE LOVERS WERE in his sights, and Eros was on the verge of letting his arrow fly when Hermes appeared, hovering in the treetops beside him. A message from Zeus, the messenger explained: *Come to the palace at once, for I wish to speak with you.* Not wanting to miss his mark, forever ruining the hearts of two innocents, Eros unstrung his golden bow and left at once.

When he arrived at Zeus's palace in the clouds, he climbed the stairs wearily. They seemed to go on forever, each one taking more effort than the last, and he considered unfurling his wings to carry him the rest of the way.

At long last, Eros found Zeus lounging in one of his many garden verandas. Long lengths of gauzy linen hung from columns, swaying gently in the breeze, as did the branches of the olive trees growing at the edges of the expansive stone patio.

Zeus kept his commanding gaze trained on Eros as he approached. When he raised his arm, Hebe, the cupbearer of the gods, appeared mid-stride with a chalice of nectar. She handed it to the god of love and smiled sweetly before vanishing.

Eros reclined on a sofa, taking a sip of the rose-gold nectar while he waited for Zeus to address him.

"I will make no pretense about why I called you here," announced Zeus, pausing to drink from his own cup. "I have seen your mortal lover. She is beautiful, with a tender heart and a strong will. A treasure, indeed."

Eros's grip around the jeweled cup tightened, and his wings ruffled as they rose along with the hair at the back of his neck. *No. No, no, no, no.* He could not bear it if Zeus set his mind to seducing his lover, his wife... his heart.

Zeus laughed, amused at the involuntary way Eros's nostrils flared. "To help her in her quest to reach you, Eros. I do not wish to steal your treasure."

The tension in Eros's jaw loosened, though his heart still hammered.

"So fair of face yet so pure of heart," mused Zeus, staring wistfully off into the distance. "I can see why she is dear to you."

Eros held onto his cup with white knuckles. "Dear enough to make her my wife."

Zeus's gaze snapped to attention on Eros. "Is this true? I did not sanction such a thing."

Eros replied without hesitation. He would do it again in a heartbeat. "Not avowed in the eyes of the gods but bound by laws of the heart."

Zeus considered for a moment, stroking his bearded chin before speaking. "Are you aware that Aphrodite has set three impossible tasks before this wife of yours, with the promise of reunion?"

"No." The breath slipped from Eros's lungs.

Zeus tilted his head slightly, arching a brow and pursing his lips. "It is true, but the mortal has persevered. Naturally, this has irritated Aphrodite, and we all know the consequence of that."

"I know what lengths Aphrodite will go to ensure others pay the debts she thinks she's owed, all too well." Eros took a sip of nectar to calm his nerves, hoping to appear untroubled. "Yes, my mother has a vendetta against Psyche, though through no fault of hers, only perceived by Aphrodite, who is notorious for putting beauty before all else. For if there is no lust, no feminine wiles, no means with which to seduce, she has nothing." Eros shook his head, his anger growing with every word. "She raves

146

about the imperiousness of gods, and it displeases me to learn she uses me in her plot to take revenge, all the while giving lectures on the trappings of vanity and the utter uselessness of loving a mortal. Sometimes I think my mother loves no one more than herself."

"She has sent Psyche into the Underworld, for an elixir from Persephone," said Zeus, nodding. "It is under the pretense of being the last and final request. I well know the game Aphrodite plays, but I have done what I can without upsetting the gods and goddesses who await judgement regarding their petty grievances. I can do no more. It is up to you now, Eros."

Eros leaned forward, regarding Zeus's words carefully. There had been whispers that some of his fellow gods had taken pity on Psyche, but Eros had dismissed them as rumors. Aphrodite had agreed to leave Psyche to her misery. Eros had no reason to believe his mother would not hold true to her word. Clearly, he did not know the depths of her hatefulness.

And now, according to Zeus, the trials had been truth. Psyche had been put through unimaginable tribulation, ending in a trip to the Underworld for believing in the word of a goddess.

How desperate had Psyche been if she had been willing to sacrifice her life for love?

Not desperate, broken, and because of him.

Eros nearly dropped the chalice. What a fool he'd been to abandon the most unconditional love he'd ever known. He was incomplete without her. Even Zeus himself was rooting for them, risking an upset in his immortal kingdom to tug on the strings of fate to bring heart and soul together once more.

The embers of Eros's love for Psyche relit, engulfing his heart, even as pride turned his passion to shame, setting fire to his face. He had turned his back instead of listening. Yet, despite his rashness, she bravely risked life and limb—and the wrath of a vengeful goddess—to find him. She had agreed to walk through fire and brimstone even if it meant being sent away, or worse, dying.

It was often discussed among the inhabitants of Olympus that human beings were feckless and weak creatures, laughed over what gullible imbeciles they were. Qualities his mother doubtless thought of Psyche. What irony it was that it was he who was weak. Him who was the coward.

Zeus's booming voice pulled Eros from his thoughts. "Take your leave, then, fly to the Underworld as fast as you can if you wish to save her. I fear she already treads that dangerous ground. I have given her the special coins the ferryman requires for safe passage of the living." Zeus took up his cup again. "The miserable wretch will not toss her into the Styx, not with the coins that bear my markings, but crossing the Styx without the souls of the damned trying to drag her under will be the least of her troubles."

Zeus held out his free hand, offering to take Eros's cup. "Go now, Eros. Save your treasure before it is too late."

Eros rose to his full height. Tall and strong and breathtaking—and deeply in love. His wings spread, and he had no more than handed his cup to Zeus when they launched him into the sky.

CHAPTER 20

AFTER A WHILE, Psyche was able to walk instead of crawl. She made her way through the narrow passage, dodging ugly winged creatures she could not name. When she finally came to an opening, she stepped out cautiously, her eyes widening when she saw what stood before her; a great ebony palace towering in the distance.

The notion that she had traveled through an artery to arrive at the lifeless heart of the Underworld was not lost on her.

She drew closer to the bridge that spanned a bubbling moat of lava, admiring how it cast an orange glow over the obsidian, when she heard an awful sound.

A three-headed hound slowly emerged from behind one of the massive stalagmites that rose from the ground on either side of the bridge. It was larger than anything Psyche could have ever imagined. Six sinister eyes peered down at her. Three fanged jaws snapped open and shut. A chorus of threatening growls vibrated in its chests.

Cerberus. Guardian of the gates of Hades.

One of the hound's heads unleashed a ferocious roar, a warning that she should not take one step closer if she valued her life. The ground beneath her shook, leaving her no choice but to sprint forward in order to dodge the avalanche of rock and debris that fell from above. Another of the hound's heads snarled in fury, and she clapped her hands over her ears, hoping her head—and her heart—would not burst.

Slumber comes when the wind blows.

Psyche groaned. Now was not the time to be thinking about riddles and rhymes.

Making your wish come true in dreams.

An image suddenly came to mind; the reeds swaying in the breeze, singing the wind god's song to bring Chrysomallus to his knees.

With her hands still over her ears, Psyche began to sing a sweet lullaby from childhood, one her mother had taught her. She sang the first verse, and when the terrifying sounds of the beast stopped, she peeked up to see all six of the hound's ears pricked and listening. This time, a chorus of whimpers came from its chests, tormented low whines that meant it was caught between protecting its master and curling up to sleep before his gate.

Psyche sang louder, her voice high and sweet, until the hound sat, one head drooping, one yawning, and the other desperately trying to shake off its growing drowsiness. She could see the guardian's attempt was to no avail, and so she sang for her life, for a life with Eros, and when that song ended, she sang another until every one of Cerberus's heads were lying on the ground soundly asleep.

Psyche continued her song, even as she crept by the slumbering hound of Hades, of which she dared to stroke one enormous muzzle as she passed. She sang with a smile as she stepped onto the bridge, breaking out into a run so the hot stone would not burn the bottoms of her feet, and almost danced to her own tune when she entered the palace of Hades and Persephone.

The king of the Underworld and his bride had been surprised to see her when she had wandered into the great room in which they dined. So much so, Hades had stood abruptly, flying out of his cushioned chair with such force that it tumbled backwards. His broad chest, clad in black silk embroidered in gold, heaved when his questions burst from his mouth like a flame.

"What is the meaning of this? Who are you? What do you want? *How did you get past my gate?*"

Psyche stood frozen, wide-eyed and trembling. Persephone sat calmly through Hades' tirade, as if such outbursts were a common occurrence. His face was red with rage, but she sat beside him serene, with inky dark hair and skin as glowing and translucent as a pearl, looking every bit of the royalty she was.

"Sit, my love. We have nothing to fear. She is a mortal."

Hades exhaled, begrudgingly giving in to his queen and retrieving his chair. Once seated, Persephone motioned for Psyche to sit as well. She did, but when Persephone invited her to dine on the scrumptious food laid out on the table before them, Psyche shook her head.

As tempting as it was, Psyche knew the truth. She'd been told the story of how Hades had tricked the innocent Persephone into eating a pomegranate, thus making is so the goddess he had fallen in love with could never leave his side. A compromise had eventually been agreed upon, and the daughter of Demeter was allowed to spend half of each year above but must spend the other half below.

"Very well," said Persephone, scattering Psyche's thoughts. "Let us start with your name. Then, why you sit before us, since your journey cannot have been without danger. What is it that has made you risk your mortal shell?"

"I am called Psyche, and it is love that has brought me here."

Hades and Persephone exchanged a look. "Come now, Psyche, it cannot be that simple," she said. "Love is complex. No one knows that better than I."

"You are right," answered Psyche, nodding politely. "The matter is not so simple. I am the wife of Eros, god of love, but I have offended him, so he has left me. I come here on a mission to win him back, to prove myself worthy, so that we may live in peace together once more."

Hades lifted a dark eyebrow, not bothering to govern the incredulousness in his voice. "The god of love has taken a *mortal* wife?"

Persephone gave Hades a pointed look. "The heart wants what the heart wants. No one should know that better than you, my love."

Reproached, Hades nodded. "So, you seek our help. What is it that we can do for you?"

"It is only Persephone who can help me. My betrothed's mother, Aphrodite, bids me to

154

retrieve an elixir, one made of the beauty of spring, for I have been the cause of much trouble. If I bring this elixir to her, she has promised a reunion between Eros and I."

Persephone stared at Psyche for a long time before speaking. There was a look of sympathy in her eyes, and a ghost of a smile that said she understood the lengths Psyche would go to and the pain she would endure.

"When I reside here, it is in the winter months," began Persephone. "Because of this, I cannot give you the elixir of spring you seek. However, I can give to you an elixir made of something equally as beautiful. Should you choose to accept this replacement, you shall have the rebirth of love you desire, Psyche."

The words had no more than left Persephone's mouth when Psyche blurted, "I accept." Whatever beauty the queen of the Underworld was willing to give, she would take it. And if Aphrodite refused it, no matter, Psyche had brought it to her. It would be no fault of Psyche's if Persephone's elixir was nothing more than muddy river water. The grudge would be between the two goddesses.

"Have you anything to carry the elixir?" asked Persephone.

After opening her satchel, Psyche withdrew the jar containing the water from the Styx. Then she rose from her seat, and, holding it carefully in both hands, placed it in front of Persephone.

Persephone reached for the jar. With elegant fingers, she uncorked it and poured the black liquid into the chalice she had been drinking from. Psyche watched silently, afraid to witness the goddess's power at work. It seemed not meant for human eyes, and she wondered if there would be consequences of carrying the knowledge with her back to the world of the living.

A chill swept through the air as Persephone circled a hand over the rim, and though tiny flakes of snow swirled around the goddess, she remained unbothered.

Psyche shivered uncontrollably, the tip of her nose growing cold, her fingers and toes tingling from numbness. Ice crystals formed on every surface, coating it with a sparkling frost, the sight as breathtaking as a frozen winter twilight.

Hades looked on with mild interest when Persephone leaned forward, closed her eyes, and blew into the cup, her breath frosty in the cold air. When she was finished, she poured the elixir into the jar, spilling not a single drop, and handed it to Psyche.

Psyche bowed, grateful for the goddess's help, and also the returning warmth. "Thank you. I hope we meet again one day, though, no offense, not too soon."

Persephone smiled. "No offense taken, Psyche. Hades and I wish you well."

She nodded her respects and then turned to leave, hurrying through the vast dining hall without further ado. She hoped Persephone meant what she had said, for Psyche new all too well the revenge goddesses were capable of.

CHAPTER 21

PSYCHE RAN PAST the still sleeping Cerberus and shimmied into the crack in the wall from which she'd come. She retraced her steps through the passage, feeling her way along the walls for what seemed like hours. When she could no longer walk, she crawled, until she came to the spot she had escaped from the cyclops. She rested on the rock that had hidden her, giving her enough time to come up with a plan.

She pushed away from the rock, stomach rumbling from hunger, muscles exhausted and aching. But she would not stop. Could not. She would deliver the jar of Persephone's beauty elixir as promised.

When Psyche finally emerged from the Underworld it was night. She sucked in the cool, fresh air in gasps. It smelled of algae and wet rock, but after the oppressive heat of the Underworld, she could not get enough.

Her head throbbed and her legs shook as she made her way along the river. Needing to rest again, she all but collapsed. Waiting for her breathing to steady, she peered out across the motionless black water, at the silvery moon reflected upon it.

She thought of the moment she would gaze up at her love's face again. Would he be happy to see her? She wished she had a cleaner dress for their reunion, one that wasn't torn to shreds.

Without thinking, Psyche crawled on scuffed knees to the edge of the river. She lifted her hand to dip it into the water, to wash her face, and bathe, perhaps, if the water did not burn her skin. But she stopped, taken aback by what she saw.

The light of the moon illuminated her once beautiful face, now smudged with dirt and, worse yet, deeply grooved with age. Her hair, once the rich color of chestnuts, was streaked through with gray and tangled.

Who was this unfamiliar woman staring back at her from the dark depths of the river?

Psyche's throat swelled, her ears burned, and her eyes stung. All the hurt and anger and frustration rose within her at once, bursting forth in a scream. She cried and wailed at her reflection, and it lamented with her, at the utter uselessness of their efforts.

The Underworld had stolen her youth, that was plain to see, and Aphrodite would have known that wretched place would do so. Psyche had not been cunning enough to look past the goddess's appeasing words to see the truth of them. She had been too confident she would not be deceived. She had foolishly thought if she did all that was asked of her, she would be worthy enough not to be told lies—to not be manipulated yet again.

Psyche sobbed, pitiful and weak even to her own ears. But she could not help it, the irony was too great, the powerlessness of her mortality too much to bear. *She* had been the elixir of beauty from which Aphrodite had selfishly taken.

Psyche threw herself away from the horrid sight with such force it felt as though she might have cracked every one of her feeble bones. The jar of elixir flew out of the satchel and, though growing less agile by the moment, she scuttled after it, so it would not shatter against the rocks. She reached it just as it came to a wobbling stop and snatched it up. She held it to her breast, cradling it against her heart. She would still deliver it to Aphrodite, as promised. She would not risk her reunion with Eros, even if it was as an old and decrepit woman.

Once her labored breathing evened again, Psyche held out the jar, turning it in her hands and inspecting it. She wondered, as she examined the divine carvings that had appeared during Persephone's ritual, what the elixir inside would do to a mortal.

A drop, just enough to bring back the luster of her hair and erase the lines on her face. She could not bear to have gone through all she had—fought as hard as she had—only to be rejected by her lover. A god as lovely as Eros did not deserve a bride as old and haggard as she'd become, so past the prime of her youth and beauty. If he did take her back, he would only do so out of pity, and that was the hardest of her bitter realizations of all to reconcile.

Mind made up, Psyche pulled out the cork with teeth that squelched in her gums and spit it into a withered, age-spotted hand. But before she could bring the rim to her lips, the jar expelled a cold, gray mist.

Stinging ice crystals blew into her face, stealing her breath. The wind whipped her hair, whistling as it swirled around her, and even through the snow she could see that it was the rich color of her youth. She smiled when she saw that her hands where once again smooth and no longer wrinkled, but her smile vanished when the jar fell from her numb fingers and shattered to pieces.

All her former glory had been restored, but she was dying in exchange. Another bargain struck, though unwittingly. Psyche thought this as she watched her skin turn a grayish blue, feeling the burn of frostbite slowly consuming her. The tears on her cheeks dropped like glittering diamonds into her lap. She tried to catch them, but she could no longer move.

One last realization struck Psyche as her head touched the ground. There was one thing the gods and goddesses could not take away from her, one thing she would hold onto as she succumbed to the deathly sleep of winter.

She had lived knowing true love. Even with the bitterness and pain and sorrow that had come with losing it, she would die a thousand times over to have known it than to have never known it at all.

CHAPTER 22

EROS DOVE FROM the sky when he spotted her. His feet hit the ground running when he called her name and she did not answer. Time stilled as he stood over her body, every smile she'd ever graced him with flashing through his mind as he knelt to gather her into his arms.

He tried to stand but sank to the ground under the weight of his sorrow and pulled her closer to him instead. Her skin was as cold as ice, and her lips were blue, a beguiling shade under any other circumstance.

"Psyche," he said, shaking her gently. "Psyche, I'm here. It is Eros. Wake up. I've come for you. I've come to take you home." He folded her tighter into his arms, wrapping his wings around them both, rocking her and stroking her hair. "Wake up. Please wake up."

When she still did not answer, his worst fear came crashing to the surface. It poured out of him in the most desperate and mortal of ways, in a torrent of hot tears streaming down his face. He had never cried before, and it was a strange and terrible sensation.

Suddenly, another emotion rose, one the gods knew all too well. He lifted his head toward the sky and screamed. "Mother!"

He spied the shattered remnants of the jar. Reaching out his hand, they reassembled themselves and flew into his open palm. He studied the markings, the signs and symbols of one of his own kind.

"Oh, Psyche," he whispered. "I would have taken you back just as you were. Every wrinkle, every gray hair, every old, brittle bone. It is your heart I love, my beautiful butterfly."

He looked up to see Aphrodite standing before him, summoned to answer for her dastardly crime. He flung the jar at her, but it sailed through her likeness to rebreak on the rocks behind.

"You knew Persephone would give her the beauty of winter instead of spring. You *knew*, and you sent her anyway. Is your vanity so great, your pride so lofty? Your love for me so low?"

Aphrodite opened her mouth to speak.

Eros's wings opened with a forceful snap, drowning out any sound that may have escaped her mouth. They brought him to his feet in one great movement as he looked down at his wife's lifeless body in his arms. A renewed wave of sorrow crumpled his face as he cried again for the loss of such a precious life.

"She was ten times more worthy of worship than you." His wings arched high above his head, ready to carry him away.

"Eros," began Aphrodite. "I can see now how much this mortal meant—"

"No. Not another word." Never in all of his life had he loathed another as much as he did Aphrodite at that moment. "There is nothing you can say. Nothing. You are no mother to me."

Eros knelt, gathering Psyche into his arms before launching into the sky. He didn't know where he would go, only that he must leave. He wept, looking down at his beloved and letting his wings carry him. When he finally looked up, he found himself at the gates of Zeus's palace.

The gates opened, and there stood Athena, as though she had been waiting for his arrival.

"Come. Zeus is expecting you," she said somberly, gesturing toward a set of gleaming marble stairs.

It seemed the others had caught wind of what had happened as well, the details no doubt divulged by Hermes, and they ascended at varying distances behind Eros as he climbed the stairs. He paid them no mind, but truth be told, he was heartened by their assemblage.

When all were gathered in Zeus's council room, the seats at the round table of the Olympians filled save for one—Aphrodite— Eros finally spoke.

"My king," he began, his voice cracking with emotion. "I was too late."

"Yes, I can see."

"Bring her back. Please. I beg you. She did not deserve this. Her death falls on my shoulders. To atone, I will give her up. Mnemosyne can wipe away all memory of me, so that she may live the life she was meant to live."

Zeus looked around the table, meeting eyes with each of the gods and goddesses in attendance. They all nodded their heads. Even Ares, the god of war.

"Very well," announced Zeus. "We are all in agreement. Psyche shall be reborn."

"Thank you."

"For it to be done, you must kiss your bride one last time."

Without hesitation, Eros bent down and tenderly kissed Psyche's lips. "Such a bittersweet thing to say goodbye, my love," he whispered, caressing her cheek one last time.

It was just then that Psyche's eyes fluttered open, and, blinking up at him.

"Eros?"

She stirred in his arms, her skin warming until a glowing golden aura enveloped her. Eros set her on her feet, for he had to, so that the delicate butterfly wings unfurling from her back had the room they needed.

"Eros. Forgive me," she said in a near breathless rush. "I promise with all my heart I will never break your trust again. Ever. I have survived terrible dangers to prove my love for you, and I would endure them all again if it meant you would come back to me."

Eros's breath hitched. How could he have ever left her?

"I never truly left, my love," he said, opening his arms so she could fall back into them without haste. "Oh, my gentle soul, my newly born goddess, I never truly left."

She looked up at him and he smiled down at her.

The loud clap from Zeus turned every head his way. "Cups, Hebe! Cups for everyone. Demeter, Athena, Artemis! Attend to the bride, for this evening heart and soul shall be bound as one in the eyes of the gods."

Eros nodded at Zeus, for it was the only way he could thank his king at that moment. It seemed the love he'd been rooting for had won, and Psyche's memory would not be wiped away, and an immortal union would take place instead.

"*Now* the prophecy is fulfilled," she said, quirking her mouth.

"So it is," replied Eros, smiling in the certainty their fate had indeed come to pass.

Psyche giggled, delighted at being led away by her fellow goddesses to prepare for her wedding and not her funeral.

Eros accepted the cup from Hebe, and the congratulatory pat on the back from Dionysus, feeling more whole than he had ever felt in his long and divine life.

They had been made for one another, he and Psyche. Heart and soul would forever be entwined from this day forward. One needing the other to create true and everlasting love.

THE END

GET A PREVIEW OF THE FLOWER AND THE FLAME

Hades had grown accustomed to living in darkness. In fact, after ruling over it for so long, he preferred it, which was why he found it so curious he would be drawn to such light. That time after time he would venture out of the shadows and into the land of the living just to catch a glimpse of it. So radiant, so warm, so bright.

But here he was, yet again.

He cocked his head, staring at her from the shadows, the girl with the sky in her eyes and the flowers in her hair. To her, he appeared as an enormous black wolf, cautiously watching from a distance. How long had it been since her singing had stopped him in his tracks one early summer morning? At least two full moons now.

Though he never hid, he was careful not to stray too far into the meadow in which she picnicked or gathered flowers. It was true the shadowy tree line concealed his dark fur, but she always knew when he was there.

She would smile when she tried to coax him out, to come closer to her. The other forest animals went to her without much convincing at all, and he longed to be near her just as they did, but that would not end well. She might see his eyes, and how they held the same piercing intensity whether he took the shape of a wolf or a man.

A god.

He also might be tempted to speak. Though shrouded in a cloak of fur and claw, a wolf capable of speech would surely give away his immortal identity. He could not have that. The King of the Underworld was not favored among the goddesses of Olympus. As maddening as it was how they made their assumptions about him, there was nothing to be done. If they chose to see fire and flames in his eyes, fury in his heart instead of loneliness, then what could he do?

So, he relied upon the dark gazing pool in his realm, waiting for its magical reflection to show him when the goddess with hair the color of sunlight had entered the meadow once again. On those days he would shift into a wolf, coming up from below to sit and watch as she laughed and sang with the nymph companions her mother, Demeter, goddess of the harvest, had commanded to keep watch over her.

Hades doubted the task was a difficult one. He found Persephone to be an utter delight, not only to gaze upon, but to listen to. She sang often, and it had been her voice that had first caught his attention, while on one of his rare trips above ground. He could not remember the reason for his sojourn. Most likely some matter on Olympus, or perhaps it had simply been a whim for cooler air, but he'd heard Persephone before he saw her, voice like the freshest of breezes. When he did see her, that smile, oh how it shined brighter than Helios.

He whined, low and pitiful, the urge to go to her growing unbearable. He wondered how long he would be able to keep up this charade when a thought came to mind. Perhaps he should try disguising himself as an ordinary man. A passerby on his way to some temple. At least that way he could get closer to her. He could speak to her, if only to ask for directions to the nearest *polis*, or some other menial thing. A whimper caught in his throat, his contemplation overwhelming him. Having had enough torture for the day, he rose quietly, turning so he could head back to his domain undetected.

Persephone stopped singing, and then, quite unexpectedly, he heard her say, "Oh, do not go yet, my friend."

Hades froze, torn between darting away and bolting towards her. Ever so slowly, he turned his massive head in her direction. She took a step forward, hands clasped together just below her throat, no doubt hoping this would be the day that she would finally convince the black wolf to come to her.

The nymphs looked on for a moment—some in horror, some in dismay—before managing to shake themselves out of their stupor. When she leaned forward, as though to take a step, they grasped and pulled on her arms, desperate to stop her from advancing any further.

Hades knew the fear squeezing the air from the lungs in their chests was from the hope that today would *not* be the day their mistress made friends with a giant beast. Demeter was fiercely protective of her daughter, and if Persephone were to be torn apart by an unnaturally large black wolf under their care, they would surely suffer a most terrible consequence. He must go, lest Persephone break free from their clutching hands and come to him.

Before he turned to leave, Hades raised his muzzle into the air and let out a long and suffering howl, even though there was no moon or a single star in sight.

Hades sat upon his throne, restless and possessing no knowledge of anything he could do to ease his torment. His seat of power was grand, carved of obsidian veined with pure gold. The room itself was large enough to accommodate a company of soldiers, yet its dark stone walls somehow seemed to be closing in on him.

Several days had passed, and he had tried to leave Persephone to her dancing and singing, to life as she knew it. Pure and peaceful. But knowing she was there, gracing the world above with her beauty and light, drove him to madness. It seemed he was doomed to dwell in the darkness; in a world where light did not exist. This did more than drive him mad, it haunted him.

He shifted when a swirling black mist rose from the tiled floor, blending into the surrounding darkness. Had it not been for the hammered copper braziers and elaborate chandelier to illuminate his surroundings, Hades wouldn't have noticed it at all.

There was a grand stone arch through which all visitors entered, yet Hecate, goddess of magic, the night, and the moon, chose to appear directly before him.

Like Hades, Hecate was neither benevolent or malevolent, yet carried with her a reputation that made gods and man alike quake at the mere thought of her. All except Hades, for Hecate and he were kindred spirits, and she often visited him in the Underworld to give him counsel.

"Receiver of Many," she greeted, floating closer. Her raven hair rippled in an unseen wind, the pointed ends of her black gown twisting and reaching like tentacles. "I do not think I have ever seen you so distressed. What vexes you?"

"Unrequited love, Hecate," replied Hades, not bothering to hide the truth from the witch. "Is there anything in existence more torturous?"

"Love? For whom?" asked Hecate.

"Persephone, daughter of Zeus and Demeter."

"I see," said Hecate. "A most difficult situation, then, for the ruler of death and darkness to long for one who brings such life and light."

174

Another confession poured out of him, unbidden. "I appear to her as a wolf when she is with her nymphs in the meadow, just to be near her. I can think of nothing else."

"Ah! Then she does not know of your love."

Hades slumped further down into the plush cushion of his throne. "I have not had the courage to tell her my darkness pines after her light, so she does not. And what would she do if she did? Is there any above or below who have not heard of the terrible god Hades? The sinister purveyor of death. Tell me, who does not cower in fear at even the thought of my name?"

Hades pushed himself up and stalked over to an ornate granite fountain holding a pool of still, dark water.

"I see." Hecate glided to where he stood, the rolling fog that forever accompanied her moving with her. "The judgement that you should preside over the souls of the dead has caused you to lose as much as you've gained. But, after all that has been said and done, you are still a king. You can simply take the girl for your own."

"There would be no honor in that," replied Hades, not giving the witch any more leave to fill his head with terrible ideas. Ones that would not bode well for his already infamous reputation, which existed thanks to the unfounded presumption that he was the perpetrator of many diabolical offenses.

"Always one so willing to suffer in the name of honor, Hades. I fear following rules, giving respect where it is oftentimes undue, is the sole source of your misery."

Had she not heard the words that had come out of his mouth?

"I do not wish to frighten her, or force upon her a life she does not want."

"I have looked where no one else has dared," Hecate continued, "into that black depth, and I have found a warm and caring soul in you, Receiver, though your mind broods over the careless misdeeds of gods and man. So misunderstood are you."

She grew larger in size, cresting like a dark wave before breaking into a cascade of smoke, and the whisper of *I know the feeling* echoed in Hades' ears as her ghostly figure reassembled to hover beside him.

Hecate looked down into the same dark pool, at the same image of Persephone as he did now, and said, "It is wise to let her choose. But first she must have something from which to make her choice. Love cannot grow from nothing. There must be soil in which to plant the seed. Go to her, offer her your heart, black as it may be, for the most fertile ground is always the darkest."

Hades contemplated this as he watched Persephone's reflection splash in a stream, laughing and giggling with sheer delight. Would he steal her happiness just so that he may find his?

"Speaking of honor," murmured Hecate, interrupting his thoughts, yet again. Clearly, the witch was not done with the conversation. "Has the great and powerful Zeus given you what you are owed for so steadfastly governing those who no longer walk the Earth?"

Hades shook his head. "I have not yet asked for his word to be honored."

Zeus had promised him a bride long ago, when Hades had agreed to rule over the dead. He hadn't wanted such a realm, one of darkness and despair, but he hadn't had a choice. Poseidon had already been granted the seas, and Zeus, of course, had claimed the heavens and Earth for his own. What was left for the third brother but to rule over imprisoned Titans and the souls of the dead?

"You have a good heart, Hades. You deserve a queen who lights it afire. Perhaps it is time for that brother of yours to make good on his debt," said Hecate before vanishing, leaving no trace she had ever been there except for a curling wisp of smoke.

The Author

Forever a fan of fairytales, folklore, and mythology, Kerri brings life to the mythological characters you know and love... or love to hate.

Kerri lives in Michigan with her husband, son and cat they lovingly but aptly refer to as The Maleficence. Mel for short. If Kerri isn't raking leaves or shoveling snow, she's either reading, writing or has fled her evil to-do list and fallen down an Internet rabbit hole... Or possibly just fallen and can't get up.

For news and updates about upcoming releases, sign up for Kerri's newsletter at kerrikeberly.com. For an inside look at the day in the life of a crafty crochet-addicted, DIY-loving, Greek mythology-obsessed author, follow her on Facebook, Instagram, and TikTok.

Milton Keynes UK
Ingram Content Group UK Ltd.
UKHW050757160424
441246UK00001B/13

9 781958 354667